The Spider's Banquet

To Mary and Paul
from the author(!!)

Jeremy

11 March 2009

The Spider's Banquet

Julius Falconer

PNEUMA SPRINGS PUBLISHING UK

First Published 2009
Published by Pneuma Springs Publishing

.

Cover design, editing and typesetting by:
Pneuma Springs Publishing

A Subsidiary of Pneuma Springs Ltd.
7 Groveherst Road, Dartford Kent, DA1 5JD.
E: admin@pneumasprings.co.uk
W: www.pneumasprings.co.uk

All the characters in this book are fictional –
except one, who knows who she is.
To her
I respectfully and affectionately dedicate this volume.

Julius Falconer

One

My name is Stan Wickfield, and I am – that is to say, I was, until I retired a year or two ago – a detective inspector in the Worcestershire CID. The story I am about to tell you has never been told before, and you seem a likely person to be the first to hear it: someone of understanding and insight who will not judge me harshly because I took so long to solve the crime. However, I must tell you the story in my own way. If I related the facts as one would expect from any self-respecting chronicler, that is to say, in chronological sequence, even you would wonder how I could be so obtuse; so I shall instead tell you the story as it presented itself to me, and my hope is that you will find yourself as baffled as I was. Then you will sympathise.

I should perhaps add that this was my first case as a newly promoted detective inspector. I thought at one stage that my promotion would be jeopardised by my incompetence, and I should not wish you to imagine that *all* my cases have been conducted so haphazardly! You shall, however, judge for yourselves. At this time I belonged to the Warwickshire force, and my wife, Beth, and I were living in Leamington Spa.

Since the convoluted affair hinges on a missing quilisma, I shall take the liberty first of all of telling you what a quilisma is. You have no need to blush for your ignorance: I had never heard of one before either! It all had to be explained to me. Please bear with me, therefore, if I start with an explanation of plainchant without which this story will not fully make sense. Plainchant, or plainsong, or

7

Gregorian chant, is, as I was told, the style of singing which evolved in the Middle Ages and was adopted by the Roman church: essentially one line of melody sung in unison, generally without accompaniment. We – you and I - are interested both in the singing and in the notation, the way it was written down. The mediaevals apparently elaborated a system of notes – or *neums*, as they were called – the groupings of which were all given one of nearly thirty labels. (That should probably be *neumata*, but let us spare ourselves the morphology!) Thus a basic note on its own was a *punctum*. Two notes in rapid rising sequence were a *podatus*, or in a descending sequence a *clivis*. A group of three descending notes, the first of which carried the accent, was a *climacus*, while a group of three equal notes, the middle one of which was one pitch higher than the outer two, was a *torculus*. And so on. You get the idea, I am sure. The other groups had such splendid names as *epiphonus, cephalicus, scandicus flexus* and *climacus resupinus* – as I say, some twenty-seven in all. If you have never seen plainchant written down, this is what it looks like:

It all looked very strange to me the first time I saw it – the same, probably, as it does to you if this is the first time you have seen it. It makes more sense to me now, of course, because of the expert – professional, you might say - tuition of which I was the beneficiary, so let me tell you just a little more about it. The mediaevals evolved a system of notation which was based on a stave of four lines (with the addition of a single ledger line above or below if required), on the lines of which, or in the spaces of which, all the notes are placed. The *melody* is indicated by neums placed higher or lower on the stave; the *rhythm* by the length or format of the neums. Flexibility is obtained by placing the note C or the note F on different lines of the stave, while the only accidental in use is the flat. The important point is the clarity of the text. Ah, you say, that sounds very straightforward and perfectly simple. Well, it does, of course, but then you have to realise that, in the absence of all our modern musical markings, the unwritten rules are extremely complex, and much more is left to the experience and intuition of the performers. So it is not nearly so simple as it looks! Indeed, the more I was told, the less I understood, so I am going to leave our music lesson there – for the moment.

You are now wondering where such esoteric lore impinges on a criminal investigation. It all began when we were called in to investigate the disappearance of a young woman at the Monastery of Our Lady of the Snows a few miles outside Coventry. The call came from the girl's sister, who was worried because she had apparently vanished during a visit to their brother, who was a monk at the monastery. She had herself dropped the girl off at the gatehouse and seen her enter the main door. Since then, nothing. She had phoned the abbot, but he could tell her nothing. She had then called in person, was of course forbidden entry to search the premises, but was assured that her sister had left within an hour of her arrival. I was courteously received by the abbot, although it transpired in the course of our initial conversation that he had absolutely no information to offer. However, he was quite willing to accompany me round the abbey, and as we went, he explained the lay-out and history of the place.

Our Lady of the Snows was a Gilbertine foundation, the only one left in the world after the upheavals of the Reformation, when the other twenty-six houses, all in Britain, surrendered peacefully to Henry VIII and his bailiffs. Gilbert, the founder of the Order of Sempringham, or Gilbertines, had set up the order in 1130, in East Anglia, primarily as a nunnery, but he had then found himself more or less obliged to instigate a parallel order of monks to ensure divine service and spiritual direction for the nuns. In addition to fully-fledged nuns and monks, there were eventually lay sisters and lay brothers who were responsible for the more mundane tasks associated with the smooth running of a self-sufficient community. The female and male members of the order resided in adjacent premises and shared a church divided down the middle. The Cistercian Rule was adapted to accommodate nuns and was finally approved by the pope in 1150.

Members of the order wear a black robe with a white cowl and a white scapular. Life revolves round the Benedictine activities of manual labour, study and prayer, with a small provision for community leisure. The purpose is threefold: to maintain a stable and predictable routine which frees the mind for spiritual exercise; to be self-sufficient and thus avoid being a burden on the local community or the wider church; and to be useful to the surrounding area by offering spiritual succour, hospitality to travellers and an example of simple living. To an observer who appreciates the value of simplicity of life-style, holiness, scholarship and the utility of prayer, the monastic life is self-evident. To us in our more sceptical age, objections are more numerous. However, although as a detective inspector I have absolutely no axe to grind, you are not listening to me to hear an apology – or otherwise - for the religious life!

Our Lady of the Snows had the typical monastic layout, the abbot told me. The church ran from west to east. On the north side was the cloister, off the west end of which branched the chapter-house. Above the cloister were the sleeping quarters, each monk having his own cell and bathroom – twentieth-century innovations, I need not tell you. Surrounding the cloister were various offices, the library, the scriptorium, the refectory. The abbey was surrounded by an enclosing wall, wherein lay the kitchen garden and orchard. Unlike other Gilbertine foundations, Our Lady of the Snows had always been exclusively for men, and a small number at that: eighteen monks maintained there an unobtrusive life struggling with the challenge of making themselves aware of the proximity of an intangible God in a world of adversity. As I came to appreciate, the monastic life is not for the faint-hearted: only the thoroughly disciplined can cope with the routine, the lack of female company, the uncertainties and aridities of the spiritual odyssey to which each monk feels himself called.

The whole was situated in a gloriously wooded valley, down the middle of which runs a stream and a country lane. From almost every vantage point, huge banks of native trees stretch upwards to the heights of the dip, cocooning the valley in a more gracious past. The monastery had originally run a flour-mill, but the building had, by the time of my visit, long since disappeared. At one point to the north of the monastic buildings, a fish-pond had been created in the stream to provide variety of diet and food appropriate to Fridays and Lent and other fasts. The valley was in theory accessible on foot through the woods, except that, in the absence of paths, the way through the thickets of brambles and nettles was not particularly inviting; and by road on a meandering tarmacked lane that joined the village of Baginton and Ashow five miles away.

There were two foci to the monastic year: the seasons, which dictated the activities in the kitchen-garden and on the abbey farm, the need for heating and lighting, the calls on the guest quarters; and the liturgical year, from Advent and Christmas, through the austerities of Lent, to the joys of Easter and Pentecost, the whole punctuated by various secondary feasts.

The day starts early with sung psalms in the chapel; a further time for sleep; more chapel; breakfast. Then come chores in the laundry, book-bindery, honey-bottling room and kitchen, round the estate, in the kitchen garden. More chapel. Study. Lunch. And so on, through to recreation before a supper consumed in silence to early bed after the fall of the *magnum silentium*, or great silence, in no circumstances to be broken. The so-called Divine Office is the formal side of communal prayer in the chapel, at which the monks sing their way through the 150 psalms of the Old Testament, with a few additions, in a week. Each day is punctuated by the singing of the quota of psalms laid down for that time of day: matins, lauds, prime, terce, sext, none, vespers, compline. At each office, the monks chant the psalms antiphonally, in Latin, the to'ing and fro'ing of the plainsong making for a meditative, disciplined, communal activity hallowed by centuries of use, allowing for no initiative on the part of the individual monk – which might lead to showmanship or one-upmanship – but freeing the mind, by virtue of the very regularity and predictability of the chant, for the appreciation of the presence of God. The only variation to this routine is provided by the requirements of the church's year – say, a High Mass on major feasts, as well as the usual Low Mass.

Of course, on the occasion of my first visit, all the monks looked identical, since all the visitor sees is the cowl covering a head bent in meditation and the loose sleeves concealing the hands. In the course of our inquiries, I soon came to distinguish one from the other: quite different features, and quite different personalities. An interesting bunch.

Having set the scene, and I hope thereby given you a clear picture of the circumstances in which I found myself that June morning, I come to a more detailed account of the cause of my involvement. I hope I have not bored you. A young woman called Elspeth Fletcher phoned the police to say that she was worried about her sister Audrey, aged twenty-three, who seemed to have disappeared. The call was passed to me, and I offered to go out to Miss Fletcher immediately to discuss the matter. She lived on her own in a flat in central Warwick, and I decided, largely for propriety's sake, to take a sergeant with me: my sergeant in those days was Jack Blundell, a taciturn but articulate man, of large build and fresh countenance. Miss Fletcher lived in a small flat on the third floor of a block in Warren Street. It was neat and clean and feminine, with a view of St Mary's Church from the sitting-room window. Pictures round the walls comprised mainly abstract works which made me shudder with incomprehension: if they had all been hung upside-down, I should not have known the difference – nor, I hazard, would she, but that is by the bye. There was a two-person sofa, a couple of arm-chairs, an occasional table, a guitar propped up in the corner, several piles of books; no television, as the events I am about to relate occurred before that creation became a common household item; several vases of cut flowers. Miss Fletcher offered us coffee, which we accepted, and then she told us of her concerns.

Miss Fletcher was a feast for hungry male eyes: very elegant, expensively dressed, with just enough jewellery to enhance the overall effect of financial ease without ostentation. She was of average height and build but with the pleasantest contours. Long black hair framed a smooth, round face out of which twinkled a pair of brilliant brown eyes under well-groomed brows. Her broad smile revealed perfect white teeth in two perfect rows. She set our hearts aflutter – in the most decorous way, you understand. (While we are on the subject of looks, I know you can hear me, but you cannot see me. The chronicler of some of the other cases that have come my way, Mr Julius Falconer, once described me as 'a large, florid man, balding, with bushy eyebrows and a great hooked nose. His lips were thin; his general demeanour purposeful but not without humour'. Not very flattering, would you say? In any case, I was twenty years younger than when that inaccurate description was penned. Magnanimity being my middle name, we shall let it pass. Mr Falconer also gives the impression that I am something of a bumbler, but the source of this mischievous piece of misinformation is a mystery to me, since he is as yet unaware of this, my first case.)

Audrey lived on her own in a flat on the north side of the town centre and worked as a research chemist for a pharmaceutical company in the town. It was her first job after leaving university with a degree in bio-chemistry. It so happened that the sisters had had supper together a few days beforehand, and Audrey had offered to consult their brother Jude in the monastery on matters connected with the disposal of their father's goods; the father had died three months previously, and the three children had not yet decided on what to do with certain family items. The mother had been dead for some years. Audrey had made the offer because it transpired that Elspeth was going to make a visit to the Westwood Business Park on the outskirts of Coventry to pick up some special material she had ordered, and she could give Audrey, who had no car, a lift to the monastery and a lift back. Elspeth duly picked Audrey up on the Saturday morning, dropped her off at the gate-house, waited for her to enter the monastery, and then drove on to the Park. She was a little later getting back to the monastery than she had calculated but was not at that point unduly concerned not to find Audrey waiting for her outside the monastery as agreed. She hung on until two hours had passed since Audrey's entry before she got out of the car, where she had been happily reading a magazine, and rang at the gate. A monk answered promptly, and she asked whether her sister was ready to return home. The monk knew nothing about it, but said he would go to the parlour to find whether she was still there. All visits to the monastery apparently took place in the parlour, the rest of the building, church only excepted, being *clausura* and off-limits to the public. The monk returned to say that since she was not in the parlour, she must have left. Elspeth then asked the monk to inquire of their brother at what time Audrey had left him. The monk again disappeared, leaving Elspeth in the reception-hall, and

13

returned five minutes later to say that their brother had seen his sister leave about an hour after her arrival. Could it be that she had set off on foot? Yes, agreed Elspeth, it was possible - but distinctly strange.

So she returned home and gave Audrey a ring. There was no reply. Audrey is a grown woman quite capable of organising her own affairs, and Elspeth thought she must have changed their agreed plan; or perhaps Elspeth herself had mistaken the arrangement between the two sisters. Again on the Sunday there was no response from Audrey on the phone, and Elspeth began to be seriously worried. It was not until the Monday morning, however, when Elspeth phoned her sister's work-place and found that she had not reported for work that morning, that she phoned the police. Hence my visit.

I asked for further clarification of the timings.

'What time did you drop your sister off at Our Lady of the Snows?' I asked.

'I can be fairly accurate there,' she said. 'The monastery like you to make an appointment rather than just drop in on spec, and we had agreed with Jude that ten in the morning was convenient for him since it fell between two liturgical offices. The abbot would readily release him for an hour's conversation. And we got there at just about ten o'clock.'

'How long do you think before you got back to the monastery to pick her up?'

'I was delayed, but not by much, so instead of picking Audrey up at eleven, as agreed, it was probably nearer a quarter past before I fetched up. Then, as I said, I waited some more. It was probably twelve midday before I rang.'

'Do I understand that you did not yourself speak to your brother on that occasion?'

'No,' said Miss Fletcher, 'the only person I spoke to was the monk on the door. Although he had not been the one who had admitted Audrey, he seemed eventually to know what he was talking about. He seemed quite confident that, since she wasn't in the parlour, she must have left the premises. Where else, he asked me in a

14

scandalised voice, could she possibly be but outside?'

'Could she have caught a bus?'

'Bus?' she asked, with a faint tone of incredulity. 'There aren't any.' I could almost hear her add, *sotto voce*, 'you poor sap'. 'Never have been, as far as I know. It's a very quiet road, you see, and these days there's only the monastery on it.'

'And I understand you spoke to the abbot at some stage?'

'Yes, I did, just before phoning you today. He couldn't add anything to the information given me by the monk on the door.'

After our interview with the fragrant Miss Fletcher, Blundell and I agreed that our inquiries would have to start at the monastery. I had taken the precaution of asking Miss Fletcher for a photograph of her younger sister. It was not a very recent one, she told me, but it showed what almost amounted to a younger version of herself. Audrey was posed in the ivy-clad doorway of some ancient ruin, in the company of a young man of her own age. A shaft of golden light from the evening sun brought her soft complexion into pleasing relief. The two stood there, with hands entwined, restfully sunk in the happiness of each other's company, gazing towards a horizon beyond even the skilful eye of the photographer. I had also asked Miss Fletcher for an account of the clothes her sister was wearing; what jewellery she had worn; whether she had an overcoat and a handbag; what kind of shoes. I quickly built up the picture of a young woman who would catch the eye of any male watcher except a monk: custody of the eyes, and so forth. It is said of Houdon's statue of the contemplative St Bruno in the church of Our Lady of the Angels in Rome that if Bruno had not taken a vow of silence, the statue would speak, so life-like is it. It may be so, but the overall impression given by that statue is, to my way of thinking, that of a monk lost to the pleasures and trumpery trivialities of the world. If the elegant Miss Fletcher the Younger had wandered through the corridors of Our Lady of the Snows, with or without clothes, I doubt whether any of the inmates would have noticed.

It has just occurred to me that, with all my blathering, I still have not told you what a quilisma is. I apologise. That is typical of me, I am afraid: all over the place, because my quick brain moves so fast from one object of interest to another. I jest, of course: a bumbling PC Plod, that's me, but as long as the Force gets there in the end, despite having me as its insignificant agent, it does not seem to me to matter a great deal. A quilisma is in effect a trill (or mordent or turn, depending on the performer's caprice and expertise): a note in a rising sequence of plainchant on which the singer executes a tremolo. It is called a 'melodic blossom' in the manuals and is depicted on the score like a w made with curved, not straight, strokes, the last of them extended upwards. In some case the w contains three v's instead of two; or the first stroke is extended downwards as well as the last one upwards. Apparently young monks – postulants – who have not yet acquired sufficient facility with the quilisma to sing it graciously with the other members of the choir are instructed to hit the preceding note with a little more sharpness than usual and then sing the quilisma as if it were an ordinary, unshaken, note. This has the effect, not of hurrying the group of notes, which is not desirable, but of refining the sound. Incidentally, the accent falls on the second of the three syllables, and the s is sounded like a z: kwi-LIZ-mer; it comes (I was told) from the Greek kylisma, which means rolling. I shall now tell you how our investigation proceeded – or did not proceed, to be more truthful.

Two

Our investigation had perforce – or am I repeating myself? - to begin at the monastery. Accordingly, Blundell and I drove the few miles out to Our Lady of the Snows and, using the massive knocker in the form of a lion's paw – at least, that is what I took it to be - knocked at the somewhat forbidding door. We had parked in front of the fortified gatehouse, in a gravelled court, and had time as we waited to take in the scene. The tower in which the main door was set was flanked on each side by a wing of two bays. On the ground floor, mullioned stone windows, ogival in shape and partly obscured by Virginia creeper, gave the building the feel of a country house. The first-floor windows, likewise ogival, crept up almost to the roof. On our right, beyond the wing, the simple but elegant southern side of the monastery chapel gave exactly the right touch of spirituality and calm. From this side of the chapel, in a semi-circle behind us as we faced the building, flowed an expanse of lawn across which the short drive had been cut. Here and there were flower-beds and a few shrubs. If we looked beyond the monastery, we could see the banks of deciduous trees, in full leaf and glittering in the sun, clothing the sides of the valley in which the monastery was embedded. A deep and satisfying silence reigned.

The door opened slowly in response to our knock, and a cowled head asked what we desired. The monk, in the order's black and white habit, was unhurried and placid – as, I suppose, one should expect. I introduced ourselves and asked to see the head monk: I should have said 'abbot', of course, but I was at the time a little uncertain of the correct nomenclature. The monk surveyed us briefly, seemed to accept our identification, and invited us to step inside to await the abbot. We followed him across a tiled hall to a door in the right-hand wing of the gate-house and entered a room which declared itself to be the Blue Parlour. The room was comfortable and cosily furnished, but, as we learnt later, this was to do justice to the dignity of visitors, not of monks, since the latter never used it. There were exposed beams in the ceiling, a wooden floor partly spread with blue carpet, a large hearth. An occasional table held a few religious magazines and volumes. Pictures on the wall included a print of the façade of York Minster, a reproduction of one of Murillo's Virgin Marys and a portrait of Gilbert of Sempringham. A surprising touch was a glass-fronted cabinet containing some fine bone china, while, in addition to the carpet, the blue wall-paper, studded with heraldic beasts, clearly explained the room's name. The sun, just moving from south to west, shone obliquely through the window.

Presently the abbot appeared: an imposing figure, well over six feet in height, tonsured as well as balding, with a craggy face and big hands. His sandaled feet matched his considerable stature. The only item of clothing which distinguished him, to our unaccustomed eye at least, from the monk who had greeted us at the door, was a simple wooden cross hanging on his chest from a chain round his neck. His name (in religion) was apparently Donatus, but we learnt that it was customary to address him as Father Abbot – which we were happy, in the interests of public relations, to do. His age I should have put at about fifty.

'Well, gentlemen,' he said, 'it does not require the brains of St Thomas Aquinas to guess what you have called about. I shall be happy to help, but I don't know that there is anything I can add to what you probably already know from the missing woman's sister.' He spoke in a quiet, measured tone of voice, the voice of a man of study and meditation.

'No, maybe not,' I replied, 'but I need to start somewhere, and you are the obvious starting-point, as superior of this monastery. We could hardly begin elsewhere without grave offence to protocol.'

He acknowledged my little joke with a nod of the head.

'What would you like to know?'

'Tell us, if you would, exactly what happened on Saturday, in so far as you have been able to piece it together. It doesn't matter at all if you repeat what we know already.'

'Inspector,' the abbot said, 'I know so little. One of our monks, Br Jude, had asked me for permission to receive his sister concerning a family matter. I was happy to grant it, providing that the appointment did not entail missing any formal activity in the monastery. I understand that his sister, Audrey I think she's called, arrived punctually at ten a.m., conversed with her brother in this very room, and left an hour or so later. And that's all.'

'Did anyone see her physically leave the monastery?'

The abbot paused, almost imperceptibly. 'No, I don't believe anyone did.'

'How was that?'

'Well, Br Jude will tell you all this himself, but as far as I understand the matter, as Audrey rose to leave, the bell for sext rang, Brother Jude made his excuses, accompanied his sister to the front door and headed in the opposite direction to make sure he was not late for the Divine Office. No porter was on duty during sext, and it was only when the elder Miss Fletcher knocked later on that we were made aware of her concern.'

'You will understand, perhaps,' he added drily, 'that in a monastery answering the door and the phone is not our top priority.'

'Quite so,' I said. 'Have you asked the other monks whether they saw the girl at all?'

'Well, no, I haven't, as a matter of fact.'

'Why is that?' I naturally asked.

''It seemed a futile exercise, Inspector. You see, all the monks, with the exception of anyone in the infirmary, of course, would have been, and were, punctually in chapel for the start of sext. A bell rings throughout the monastery and in the gardens to alert the brothers that they need to get moving, and so everyone was in the chapel when Br Jude said goodbye to his sister.'

'I see,' I said. 'That all seems very clear. I hope you won't mind, however, if I ask around just to satisfy my curiosity.'

'I have to say, Inspector,' the abbot said with some deliberation, 'that that would be a rather unusual procedure, but in the circumstances I offer no objection.'

'Good,' I commented. 'Is there an opportunity when I can talk to the monks as a group?'

'Yes, there is. If you wait half-an-hour, we generally assemble in the refectory' – he pronounced this word with the emphasis on the first syllable of three, *more catholico* – 'for a cup of tea at four, and I should be happy for you to have a few words then. In the meantime, can I offer you a cup of tea?'

I glanced across at Blundell and saw willing acceptance in his look, so the two of us agreed.

At four o'clock, the abbot led the way to the monks' refectory – sorry, REF-ectry. This was a gracious if austere room, illuminated by tall windows on the one side and dominated by a high table where, I hazarded to myself, the abbot and perhaps two or three of the monastery's senior officers sat. Down each side of the room was a long table capable of seating ten or twelve monks. In one corner stood the only piece of ornate furniture in the room: a pulpit accessed by a short flight of steps, from which, presumably, a reader spoke during meals. As we entered, the monks were milling around in sedate silence, each taking a cup of tea and a biscuit at the hatch. Some were seated to drink, others preferred to stand. The abbot led us to the top table and invited the monks to listen to me for a few minutes. I admit I was a little embarrassed, finding myself in so unusual a position.

'Brothers,' the abbot intoned, 'Detective Inspector Wickfield, from Warwickshire CID, would like to say a few words. Inspector.'

'Er, Brothers,' I stammered, 'please forgive this intrusion on your thoughts, but the circumstances warrant it, I believe. You will all know by now, I suppose, that on Saturday Brother Jude's sister Audrey called at the monastery to see him about a family matter. She has not been seen since.'

I paused to let these sinister words sink in, and, if possible, the silence of my audience deepened. I had no idea, of course, which of them might be Brother Jude.

'We just do not know whether she left the monastery or is still here somewhere, or whether she left and has disappeared either of

20

her own accord or under some malign influence. I am speaking to you just to satisfy myself that none of you saw her or can add to what we know. Any information would be gratefully received. I have Father Abbot's permission to speak particularly with Brother Jude, but can anyone else tell us anything that you think might be useful?'

I stopped, hoping that I had recovered a measure of equanimity and conveyed my message in a suitable form. Were monks sufficiently terrestrial to focus on my question, I wondered. I was never to find out, because there was no response whatever: not a word! I thanked the company for their attention and left the refectory with the abbot and my sergeant.

Back in the parlour, Blundell and I had a brief interview with Brother Jude. He was a short-set, sturdy individual, with immobile features, hair cropped as well as tonsured. In years he was probably mid-thirties. A five o'clock shadow gave him a swarthy, and I have to add shifty, appearance, although he was possibly, I told myself, the saintliest personage this side of Istanbul. My assessment of him was later to be considerably refined – for the better, I may add.

'Brother Jude,' I began a little diffidently, 'could you just explain the system of porters at Our Lady of the Snows?'

'Yes, Inspector, that's no trouble.' His voice was educated and well-modulated,   and to my ears pleasing. Perhaps there was a warmer side to his character than appeared on the surface. 'We have no permanent porter: we are a small community, living remote and quiet lives, and there seems no point. The only people who call or phone are trades-people, and not many of those since we try to be self-sufficient, and the occasional traveller applying for hospitality. If we are expecting a caller at the door – with, say, provisions for the kitchen, or a supply of altar-wine – one of us is detailed to keep an ear out for the door-knocker. If the phone rings, any one of the monks should take it on himself to answer it. There is a primitive switchboard in the hallway, and he can easily put the message through to the guest-house or the kitchens, the abbot or the bursar, as needed; but I can imagine occasions, when we're all in chapel, for example, when a caller at the door or on the phone would receive no answer for quite some time!'

21

'Thank you for that. I have a clearer picture in my mind now. Can we come to last Saturday morning? What happened exactly?'

'There's no mystery, Inspector,' the monk replied. 'At about ten, I answered the door to my sister, only because we were expecting her. Otherwise any passing monk, had there been one, would have answered her knock. I accompanied her into the Blue Parlour, where she's been before. I then fetched a pot of tea for the two of us from the kitchen, and we talked about my father's estate - the disposal of some of my father's personal property, mainly – but then we went on to other matters. I hadn't seen my sister for some time, and we chatted about this and that: we're not precisely enclosed monks, you know.'

'Quite,' I said, to let him know that I was following his account perfectly. 'What happened at the end of your conversation?'

'Well,' said the monk after a pause, as if to recollect the facts, 'I can tell you only what I told Father Abbot that afternoon. I am a little distracted, as you will understand, to think that anything may have happened to her, particularly while she was here. When the bell went for sext, I rose, she rose. She made one or two final comments before I walked her to the front door. We said goodbye quickly, as I was about to be late, and then I went to chapel.'

'Was anyone else around?'

'No, no one.'

'A guest, perhaps? One of the other monks?'

'No, Inspector, no one at all – not even my guardian angel.'

I looked at Blundell, and, taking the hint, he quickly added a couple of questions of his own.

'Brother, did she seem perfectly normal to you?' Brother Jude's head swung round, but there was no change of expression.

'Yes, perfectly, in so far as I could tell. She certainly never said anything to the contrary.'

'Would she have told you if any matter had been particularly troubling her?'

'That's hard to tell, really,' the monk said in reply. 'There's ten years between us, but we've always got on well. Am I a sympathetic, listening sort of person? I'd like to think so. If she had anything on her mind, I think she might have come out with it.'

'Can you think of any reason, any reason at all, why your sister should have chosen to disappear of her own accord?'

'No. As I said, she seemed perfectly normal to me. As we parted, she said she was expecting Elspeth to pick her up any minute. The sun was shining, and it would have been no hardship for her to sit on a bench in front of the monastery until Elspeth arrived. In any case, a monastery is hardly the place to attempt a disappearing act!'

After we had left the monastery, really very little the wiser, I ventured to ask my sergeant what had been his reactions.

'Well, Sir.' He cleared his throat, clearly as nervous as I was on our first investigation together. I guessed that his previous inspector had not included him greatly in the lucubrations that inevitably accompany a case that is not straightforward. 'Let's suppose that Audrey Fletcher left the monastery on foot, as it seems must have been the case. There are only two ways to go, north towards Baginton, south towards Ashow. Both distances are about two and a half miles – say forty to forty-five minutes' walk on a warm June day. Now Elspeth Fletcher came from the Baginton direction, so she would had to have seen her sister if she were on the Baginton road. Ergo, Audrey walked towards Ashow. Perhaps we should instigate a few inquiries at Ashow, Sir?'

'Good, Blundell, good,' I said warmly. 'But what if she did not leave the monastery?'

'In that case, Sir, she must still be there!'

'And what are the alternatives, would you say?'

'None worth considering seriously, I venture to say, Sir. For someone on foot, there's open countryside east and west of the monastery, once you have negotiated the steep and no doubt tangled woods of the valley. And why on earth should Audrey set off on such a wild enterprise? Alternatively, a car passing her between the monastery and Ashow scooped her up. This could be a case of abduction and murder.'

'Yes, Sergeant, I agree that it is unlikely Audrey left the monastery. Why walk on a hot day when you're expecting your sister to give you a lift? But never the less I take your point that we need to do some asking-round at Ashow. That's our next job.'

Ashow is a somewhat isolated village, lying mostly off the 'main' road – which made our investigation even less likely to produce results – containing some fifty houses and a population of 140. Picturesque cottages, a post office, a twelfth-century church and adjoining churchyard, and a pub – there, in a few words, you have it. Industry? None. Work? Strictly agricultural – unless one commutes into Warwick or Coventry. With the help of an officer in uniform – *you* may call him a flattie, but I have more respect for the uniformed branch than that – Blundell and I covered the entire village in next to no time. We each carried a photograph of the missing girl and at every front-door invited information about sightings, either of the girl or of a stranger or of an unfamiliar car. Although not every householder answered our knock, even though by this time the evening was well advanced, we reckon we covered ninety percent of the village. For good measure, we left details in the pub, in the church porch and with the mistress of the post office. As I expected, our round of Ashow produced no useful information whatever. On the other hand, it is always pleasant to meet the British public in their own surroundings: the aged, the young, the friendly, the hostile, the pretty, the plain, male and female, all on their own doorsteps.

We realised also that we should have to execute the same manoeuvre in Baginton. Since it was by then too late to contemplate it meaningfully that evening, we reconvened the following morning. Baginton, rather larger than Ashow, boasts a ruined castle – well, the little that's left of it - a newish air-field – at least it was newish at the time of which I speak – a famous oak-tree and a pub named after it, and a church dedicated to St John the Baptist. None of this concerned us: busy people, policemen. Again we went round every house, many of which, it being a Tuesday morning, were empty, and again we left details of our search in likely places in the village. We had not contacted by any means every possible inhabitant, but we felt we had done our best in the circumstances. In the next few days, every villager would be aware of the police hunt for a missing girl, and if any information were available, we were confident it would come our way. In my experience, the public is, generally speaking, only too happy to assist the police.

Blundell and I called in at the station, hoping that some message, a result of our previous evening's efforts at Ashow, awaited us. Over a cup of tea, we held a brief conference. Again, I asked my sergeant for his thoughts at this juncture.

'Right, Sir. This is how I see it, at the risk of repeating myself. There are two alternatives: either Audrey never left the monastery, in which case she is still there, or she did leave. In the latter case, we have again two alternatives: either she disappeared of her own accord – people do it all the time – or she was abducted. If she disappeared of her own accord, there is probably little we can do. She has had three days to make good her "escape", as we might term it, and every opportunity to cover her tracks. If, on the other hand, she was abducted, it could only have been because she was alone on the road that runs outside the monastery. Let us agree that she left Our Lady of the Snows at eleven o'clock: this seems to be the unassailable consensus. Her sister says she arrived at the monastery to pick Audrey up at approximately eleven fifteen. This means that she would have been driving through Baginton at, say, eleven ten. At eleven ten, Audrey, on foot, could have covered little more than half a mile. The sisters therefore were bound to meet on the road. If, on the other hand, we surmise that Audrey set off towards Ashow, we need to find a reason for her to do so: and there just isn't one. It looks to me, Sir,' he added with an appropriate degree of hesitation, 'that she never left the monastery.'

'Sergeant, that's a very capable summary of the situation, if I may so without sounding patronising, and I have to say I concur in every particular. That leaves us with a very unpleasant task, I'm afraid. We are suggesting that some holy monk did away with a harmless young girl; and we shall have to turn the monastery upside-down and interview a group of holy joes to prove it. Dear, oh, dear.'

Three

However, before we could embark on that, a puzzling piece of news was relayed to us at the station. For the sake of coherence(!), I am going to give here the background to it, even though we did not discover the facts until much later. My superior thought I should be told of another missing – possibly missing - girl in the area, as it might tie in with our investigation into the disappearance of Audrey Fletcher. This is the story as he told it to me. The police station had received an anonymous call on the previous Thursday – two days before Audrey Fletcher went missing, therefore - reporting a scuffle in Chapel Street, Warwick. The informant was a respectable and reliable witness, an elderly lady minding her own business as she walked home from a Bible-study session at the local church hall. As far as she could reconstruct the action, a couple of young people walking in one direction met a single woman walking in the other. Angry words were exchanged as the parties met, the exact content of which the witness, being on the deaf side, was unable to catch, and in the mêlée one of the woman lunged with passion (to use the witness's evocative phrase) at the other. She could not at that moment of the action discern which of the two women was the aggressor, since the three actors were 'drawing apart after a scrimmage'. The other two people involved in the scuffle were said to have scattered immediately to the four winds – or two winds, I suppose would be a more accurate description - leaving the female victim, apparently dead, on the pavement. The old lady had by this time walked well past the scene of the fracas and was terrified to return to help the girl in case she was herself attacked. She thought that her wisest course of action was to make for the nearest telephone kiosk, or her own house, whichever she came to first, and report the matter to the authorities. This she did. She was happy to give her name and address, the circumstances of her presence at the scene and as detailed an account of the event as she could, in her troubled state, call to mind. However, when the police arrived, there was no sign of a body, and over the next days, no reports were made of a missing person, and there were no unexplained admissions to the casualty departments of hospitals in the area. It was all very mysterious, and it was quite some time before we found out whether the *dramatis personae* existed in reality or only in an elderly person's over-heated imagination. It was a real event, but since only one of the three people involved is directly relevant to our story, I am taking the opportunity now to tell you something about her.

Her name was Jadwiga Zawadzki, and you would not be wrong to conclude, since nothing escapes your razor-sharp intellect, that she was Polish. She was born and lived in the village of Orszewice in the Łódź region of the Carpathians, where her parents worked the land as peasants. She was the youngest of five children. Far from being spoilt, she was as lucky as the rest of the family to see meat or fish. Diet consisted largely of home-grown fruit and vegetables, and since nothing of what they ate was imported, there was a certain monotony in the diet: no oranges or bananas, for example, few spices, none of the more exotic vegetables we take for granted today. When they were fortunate enough to eat meat, it was only what the men of the family could hunt, trap or shoot, the occasional chicken from the farm, a pig once a year. Jadwiga's mother did what she could, but circumstances, and time, were against her. The family laid down food for the winter, by drying, bottling, making fruit leathers and so forth, but a long winter could be very challenging. Water was drawn from a well in the field adjacent to the house, and occasionally the well was polluted when a chicken fell in. On those occasions, Jadwiga was let down on a rope, dressed only in underwear, to remove the offending bird. Since there was no sanitation, indoor or out, the hedgerow had to serve for the satisfaction of natural needs. Sanitary towels were unheard of: scraps of paper or cloth had to suffice. Since drawing water was arduous, water was used sparingly. A wash for Jadwiga consisted of a quick wipe round the face with the dish-cloth. The family walked everywhere - no cars, no bikes, virtually no public transport - or went in a pony and trap.

Fire for warmth and cooking was provided by a wood-burning stove, and this meant arduous hours cutting down and chopping or sawing wood. Jadwiga's father, Kazimierz, would set off with the pony and cart and return hours later, often numbed with the cold, with a cart-load of logs for further chopping. There had to be enough wood stored near to the house in case of heavy or prolonged snow. He sharpened his own tools. He also made his own fences, repaired his own sheds and byres, and ploughed the fields with his own oxen. His wife, Zofia, always known as Zosieńka, milked their few cows, but otherwise spent much of her time in the kitchen-parlour preparing food or mending clothes, making baskets, knitting socks and gloves, washing clothes, looking after the children, ironing with an old smoothing-iron heated from within by live embers.

Their house consisted of three rooms on one floor. The central room was the kitchen-parlour – used by everyone all the time. On either side of it were two smaller rooms, bedrooms, one for the parents and perhaps a child if it was sick, the other for the offspring. There was therefore little opportunity for privacy. The bedrooms were lit by candle only at the moment of going to bed and were unheated. The kitchen was lit as little as possible by an oil-lamp, which made some work difficult to undertake: fine stitchwork, for example, or reading.

Orszewice is not really a village, only a hamlet, set some three hundred feet up on the lower slopes of the Carpathians. Since the village faced more or less east, the sun was soon gone in the afternoons. The Zawadzki 'farm', really just an oversized allotment carved out of the ungracious mountain, was protected by a stone wall. If crops needed watering, water had to be drawn from the well and carried up in the cart. Neighbours' 'farms' ran alongside, and the villagers helped one another out at harvest and other busy times of the year.

The community, even in Communist times, was Roman Catholic, and the highlights of the year were dictated by agricultural activity in the first place, but by the church's year in the second. Some festivals, like Easter or Pentecost, always fell on a Sunday, but others, such as Christmas or 15 August, could fall on any day of the week; in which case it was not always possible to take time off work to hitch up the trap and canter the five miles to the nearest church. However, what the family lacked in the public expression of their faith they made up for with devotions in the home: night prayers, daily rosary, novenas, the Nine Fridays. The village had a community hall where dances and similar functions took place. The nearest doctor was twenty miles away.

Life was simple. No one locked his or her house. Winter evenings witnessed an activity known as 'calling', in which one couple or family went to visit another. There was no previous announcement, no special ceremony, but the hosts would have been ashamed not to be able to offer a hot drink and a home-made cake. School functioned up to the age of eleven, when the children were expected to work on the farm. If the farm would not support them, the younger children – in most cases – as soon as they were old enough left for the nearest town to find employment; or joined the army; or became a religious. The people were poor but did not realise it. Since none or few had ever seen wealth, there was no standard of living with which they could compare their present circumstances, and most accepted their lot as human living as God intended it to be.

I now come to Jadwiga's story. I need to explain to you how it fell out that she was in Warwick – 'of all places,' I hear you say - at the time of our story, and why there was an initial mystery about her role in it. Jadwiga was nineteen when disaster struck the family. What sort of a person was she? She was pretty, vivacious, even pert, with a bold curiosity about the world around her. She combined the peasant's patient contentment and comfortable self-sufficiency with the spirited young person's desire to broaden horizons and deepen experience. She could read and write, and she had even carried on her education by herself beyond the age of eleven, within the limits, naturally, of their poverty. She had acquired the skills forced on the family – any poor family – by the need to husband exiguous resources, but, being the youngest of the family, she had not had to engage in the more arduous manual work necessary on the farm. None of the local male youth appealed to her: a parochial, pedestrian lot, she would say, stick-in-the-muds to whom she would be reluctant to tie herself for life. She was, in short, bored by the narrowness of rural life in the Carpathians in the 1950s. You and I might call that a weakness, but I am not here to judge the personages of our story, and I offer no comment.

Her chance (as she saw it) came when both her parents died within days of each other from some fever caught, it was supposed, on a market visit to the nearest town. The family were distraught. While sudden death was a hazard of rural areas, where doctors were in short supply, the death of both parents at once was rare, and for a while the Zawadzkis, albeit supported by the local clergy and the community, were in disarray. Gradually plans were formulated, the future constructed, and Jadwiga given reluctant permission to try her fortune elsewhere. The villagers and family members scraped together enough funds to enable Jadwiga to travel to Great Britain: Coventry was her goal. You may remember, if you are old enough, that many Poles came to Britain after Hitler's invasion of Poland to sign up with the Free Polish Forces, which were based in Britain. An airbase north of Coventry, at Bramcote, saw the training of Polish aircraftsmen, and after the war, refusing to return to a Soviet Poland, many of the men decided to settle in the land of their adoption – not without encountering considerable opposition in some quarters, I may add (with shame). That, however, is another story. Jadwiga had heard of a distant relation who had settled in Coventry and was apparently, if her informants were to be trusted, making a living as a factory hand - skilled jobs were closed to Poles at that time – but nevertheless better-off than under a totalitarian regime wrenching a living from an unforgiving landscape.

So it was, then, that Jadwiga Zawadzki, aged nineteen, came to Coventry in search of work, lodging and a new life in a free country still rebuilding itself after six years of near-fatal struggle. Not knowing her relative's address, she used her meagre money to rent a room in a rooming-house, and her sunny good looks soon procured her a job in a factory that made electric kettles, paid by piece-work. Repelling the owner's advances did not lose her her job: perhaps he hoped for greater success at a future endeavour. She made ends meet by a variety of stratagems. For example, on a Saturday evening, when shops closed, she would sally forth with a sack and pick out of boxes and dustbins grocery and bakery goods that the shops had discarded as unlikely to last until Monday in a saleable condition. She frequented jumble-sales and bazaars. She did odd jobs: baby-sitting, shopping for the elderly for a small emolument, bits of gardening at weekends. As the months passed, she began to be able to put aside a little money for luxuries, such as a new(ish) dress with which to go to a dance, or a slightly different hair-do. She acquired a satisfactory mastery of the English language and began to contemplate romance. Her cheerful appearance and wide smile, her natural vivacity, the exercise of her initiative and resilience, and her independent spirit had turned her into a very personable young woman – and I so wish she were not part of my story.

In time she walked out with a fellow-Pole called Henryk Krawiec, about her own age and, like her, an immigrant tempted by reports of a relative's success. They had met at the Polish church, St Stanislaw's in Springfield Road, a little to the north of the city centre. Henryk worked in a factory specialising in exhaust systems in the suburb of Foleshill – much less populated then than now, of course. In a daring move, they decided to pool their resources to enable them, in due course, to marry, and Jadwiga duly moved into Henryk's flat. Since the flat was one of scores in a slightly run-down block, nobody noticed – and would not have cared a row of beans if they had. It is neither my task as chronicler, nor in my nature as an educated, liberal, enlightened, professional, middle-class citizen (you can take some of that with a pinch of salt!) to pontificate on other people's moral or religious standards, and I comment only that Henryk and Jadwiga have my sympathy. Would you condemn them for transgressing the laws, wise and soaked in tradition though they are – and I speak as a religious man myself - of their church? Perhaps you would; that would be your prerogative. The facts are, however, whether we agree with them or not, that this little cell of two humans, man and woman, embarked on an intimate life together, clinging to each other in a spreading sea of humanity in a strange country which they had taken to their hearts.

Shortly before the start of our story, Henryk was summoned to his manager's presence and given the option of promotion. The firm intended to open a new factory in Warwick: would Henryk accept to move as a superviser?   Henryk spoke to his beloved, and they decided that he should accept.   There were a number of considerations: the expense of a move, the difficulty of finding accommodation in a town with which neither was familiar, Jadwiga's job, the difficulties of settling in a smaller place, the departure from a church whose language they shared.   In the end, they made the move, found a small flat and began a new phase of their life – only to have it disrupted by the stern and peremptory hand of fate.

Two other facts that are relevant emerged.   First of all, neither Henryk nor Jadwiga had, at the time of our story, valid visas.   Their original visas, which included permission to work, had expired with the lapse of the first year, and because they were afraid the visas would not be renewed, neither of them attempted to approach the authorities.   Secondly, Jadwiga could not find a job immediately in Warwick, although she did her best.   She remained sanguine, but employment was harder to come by than in the bigger city. You, the perspicacious Reader in the depths of your armchair, may have already penetrated with ease the implications of these two items of information, but I confess that they completely passed by me, the young inspector supposedly trained for detection.

I am constantly amazed by the contrast between the seemingly changeless lives of some communities and the jostled, turbulent lives of others.   Remote savages survive for centuries unperturbed by historical events, that is, events which shape our own narrow view of history; rural communities retain, generation after generation, customs and ways of life that respond little to upheavals elsewhere in the country or continent; to this day you can visit villages which the twentieth century, indeed the nineteenth century also, has mercifully passed by; while other communities witness events of a devastating nature which sweep away the comforting truths and life-styles of their members. Of course, there is much to be said for progress: labour-saving machines, analgesics, sanitation, running water piped into the home at the turn of a tap, and so forth, but, to my jaundiced and elderly way of thinking, much has been lost on the way.   Civilisations rise and fall – mercifully – and human lives, caught in a maelstrom of irresistible forces, are twisted and warped out of existence in the process. Life moves on, and history with it, and I am not in favour of glamorising one period of history at the expense of others as a golden age. The same may be said of individuals: some go through life without a ripple to disturb its even tenor, while for others life is a rollercoaster of unpleasant surprises and dreadful crises. However, I must curb my unfortunate and probably tedious tendency to philosophise at the drop of a policeman's helmet. Let us return to Our Lady of the Snows! (I heard that sigh of relief, Kindly Reader, but I shall choose to ignore it.)

Four

Deciding that to announce our visit beforehand, as it were forewarning the abbot that the police were about to raid his premises, would be inadvisable, I collected a small team of uniformed constables, under the leadership, if that is not too strong a word, of myself and Blundell, and we arrived the following morning with a warrant to search the abbey.

It was a warm, sunny day, a day of cloudless skies and skittish birds, woodland smells and rural peace. The scene cannot have changed much for hundreds of years: just the addition of tarmac, I suppose, to the country lane that shadows the course of the Cass stream as it winds its way down the valley to join the Ouse. I quote from John Grimham's 1761 work, *Some Lesser-Known Corners of Warwickshire* (p.71 for the studious):

> The Cass Valley is little known to any excepting the few Farmers and Labourers of the district who worship at the Abbey Church set in the heart thereof. The Woodes of native trees strech down as far as the narrowe layne, which alone stands as the Connection between the Abby and the outside Worlde. There is here a Stillnesse and a Solitude the Traveller is not likely to discover to such an extent in the County, for whiche alone it would be worth his Tyme to amble down from Baginton to Ashow on a Summer's day, imbibing and absorbing the Beauties of Nature's profusion: and perchance he may taste also somewhat of the monastic Ideals of Peace and Devotion to things of the Spirit. There is even a small but comfortable Establishment at the latter village, where he may

take refreshment in the form of Tea, and thus recruit his Strength after the exertions of his walk.

And so on, as the author enumerates some of the more unusual trees and flowers that flourish in the valley, describes a stone bridge erected by the monks of past ages to give access to abbey fields on the far side of the stream or enters a detailed description of the abbey itself.

I knocked on the imposing door, saw the look of surprise on the porter's face and entered with my team without further introduction.

'Please tell Father Abbot that I am here, Brother. In the meantime I hope you will allow us to wait in the Blue Parlour.'

The monk stammered a few words, disturbed ever so slightly in his customary self-possession by the sight of so many imposing gentlemen in uniform with such a determined figure at their head – ahem – and scuttled off, so to speak, to find his superior. The latter appeared some minutes later with a concerned look on his large face and inquired politely what it was we wanted with him.

'Father Abbot,' I said by way of reply, 'I have a warrant here to search the abbey, because we have some reason to believe that the young woman Audrey Fletcher is secreted somewhere on the premises – or perhaps in the grounds. I hope we have your permission to go where we wish, as it's important we do the job thoroughly.' I paused here to give the abbot time to consider his reply. However, he seemed to take the matter in his stride and said with no sign of anxiety or concern, 'Yes, of course, Inspector. We have absolutely nothing to hide, but I would ask that your men go about their business as quietly as possible so as not to disturb the monks at their labours.'

'Perhaps you have a map of the abbey buildings and gardens, so that we can plan our search methodically?' I asked.

'Yes, Inspector, we have. Perhaps you would be good enough to wait for a few minutes while I ask the brother procurator.'

With that, he disappeared with a quiet rustle of his habit, and we sat down in the Blue Parlour to await his return.

'Well, Inspector,' said one of the constables, 'this is a rum show.

First time I've ever set foot in a monastery, and I certainly didn't expect to be doing so in the hunt for a young woman!'

'Nor I didn't,' said another. 'Wait till I tell my missus I've spent my shift visiting an abbey!'

After a few minutes, the abbot returned with a large piece of paper which he proceeded to unfold and spread out on the table.

'Here you are, Inspector. You can see the gate-house, the church, the cloisters and all the other buildings that are home to us. Please don't force cupboards or doors: we have keys to all of them and will be happy to come round with you to make your search easier. But I think everything'll be open.'

I divided my men into four teams of two, myself and Blundell being one of them. I apportioned the various parts of the abbey so that nothing was omitted and nothing covered twice. Blundell and myself would search the church, the abbot's office, the procurator's office and the chapter-house. Team 2 would see to the two parlours in the gate-house, the guest-house behind them, the refectory, the kitchens and the honey-bottling room. Team 3 would cover the laundry, the ground-floor toilets, the library and the domestic stores, while Team 4 were responsible for the scriptorium, the printing-room, the music-rehearsal room and the fuel-store. Then Team 1 would move to the cellars, Team 2 to the monks' sleeping quarters, the infirmary, surgery and calefactory (now the recreation-room) above the cloisters, Teams 3 and 4 to the outbuildings: greenhouses, tool-shed, potting-shed, cow-shed, barn, old stables and dove-cot. Then if necessary we would have to go over the grounds.

'Men,' I said, putting on my efficient and authoritative voice for the first time in my inspectorial career, 'we are looking for a young woman, who may be alive or possibly dead, or for evidence that she has been in the monastery: clothes, jewellery, hand-bag, that sort of thing. You are to open every cupboard and every door. You are to peer behind screens and heavy furniture. You are to inspect floors and walls for signs of recent disturbance. Look in attics if there are hatches – shout for a ladder. Open chests and boxes, inspect under beds. Well, you know the routine. If that girl has come to any harm here, we shall expect every effort to have been made to conceal the fact. So be careful, vigilant and thorough. We cannot afford to miss anything. Try not to disturb the monks, but be firm – and always polite, of course. We'll meet back here in, let's say, two hours. Any questions?'

'Yes, Sir,' a member of Team 2 piped up. 'Is it all right to search the infirmary even if there are sick monks in residence?'

'Yes, you'll have to, but you'd better check with the brother infirmarian first. We don't want you catching some dreadful disease - or, on the other hand, hurrying some sick brother to his grave, do we?'

'And can we taste the honey in the bottling-room?' said his mate.

'Don't be foolish,' said I. 'This is a serious exercise.'

The search parties made a final check of their areas on the plan of the abbey and dispersed. Our sensation was a curious one. On the one hand, the abbey was undoubtedly busy, and at every corner we turned and in nearly every room we entered, there was a monk, intent on the task before him, wrapped in prayer (we supposed) but purposefully occupied. On the other, there was an atmosphere of calm which almost gave the impression that the entire building was empty.

In the kitchens, three monks were busy preparing the midday meal. They worked in silence, except for the occasional grunt from Brother Michael, the head cook. There was a stirring of pots, a peeling of vegetables, a mixing of ingredients, a walking hither and thither in the search for equipment or forgotten materials. Along the corridors, Brothers Anselm and Gerard were flicking their dusters and wielding home-produced brooms, scooping up the dust and decanting it into bags for disposal. In the procurator's office, Brother Bernard, the bursar, pored over his accounts, drew up lists of works to be undertaken on the fabric, debated within himself whether the abbey could afford this or that – at least, that is what I imagined he must be doing. In the guest-house, the guest-master, Brother Reginald, saw to it that the two guests had some sort of programme for the day, that they had everything they needed, that their spiritual needs in particular were being met. In the toilets, Brother Benedict was on his knees, scrubbing the floor. And so on. The Gilbertines, like all Cistercians, specialise in farm work, but work round the abbey was also important if the monks were not to live in squalor.

When we reconvened after our initial search, nobody had anything to report. Nothing of a sinister nature had been found. On the other hand, one or two corners had not been investigated, and the next half-hour was devoted to filling these gaps in our agenda. Still nothing.

'Right, lads,' I said, concealing my disappointment. 'There's only one thing for it: we shall have to head for the grounds. We may have to bring dogs in, but for the moment we'll try without. Let's break for lunch, and we'll meet back here at, say, two o'clock.'

The teams left in the cars to head for the nearest pubs, or possibly the station canteen. By the time we met to continue our search, it was so warm that I willingly gave permission for the uniformed men to leave their jackets in the Blue Parlour. Off we set, dividing the estate up amongst us as we had the house: the so-called abbot's garden, the herb-garden, orchard, potager, cemetery, fields, spreading out from the abbey buildings. Slowly we worked our way across the land, in pairs, this time looking no longer for a female imprisoned or hiding from us, but unequivocally for a body. Our thoughts had therefore turned from the hopeful to the sombre. We were looking for signs of disturbance of the ground. June is not the month for digging holes or turning over the soil, and I hoped that any grave, shallow or deep, would be apparent to the trained eye. Unfortunately it was. Our fears were realised when Team 3 spotted a likely site and shouted across an open field – oh, transgression! – to call me over. I agreed with them and summoned all the men. While two returned to the tool-sheds for a couple of spades, we stood around in silence, pondering the implications of our discovery. The site was in the cemetery, beside the wall, and I have to say, although it sounds very silly, that the last place I expected to find a dead body was the abbey cemetery! The men returned with spades, and the shallow grave responded to careful digging by revealing the unmistakeable remains of a young woman, fully clothed and loosely wrapped in a sheet – or perhaps I should say shroud.

I need not relate to you our sorrow, for the girl and for her family, and our anger that so young and promising a life had been snuffed out. I waited impatiently for the initial results of the autopsy, which came through on the following day, even though I was in no doubt about the basic facts. My suspicions were confirmed. The girl had died from a single stab-wound to the chest. The face was bruised from two heavy blows, which had swollen and disfigured the features, but there had been no sexual assault; and the girl had never had children. I need not therefore wait for the full autopsy results, body-part after body-part, organ after organ. When the body was presentable, I asked Elspeth and Brother Jude to come to the mortuary to identify the corpse. I thought of Tom Bowling:

For though his body's under hatches,

His soul has gone aloft.

The siblings were under no doubt that this was their sister, tragically done to death in the prime of life. I asked them what their intentions were concerning burial, thinking that perhaps interment in the abbey cemetery would be a first option. Elspeth was adamant: her sister was to be cremated and the ashes buried near those of their parents. She, Elspeth, could never imagine returning to the abbey, after these events, to venerate her sister's last resting-place. It came to pass, therefore, that Audrey Fletcher was laid to rest, at the desperately early age of twenty-three, in the municipal cemetery in Oaks Road, Warwick.

We had by that time cordoned off the entire abbey cemetery and undertaken a thorough search of the area. We were looking in particular for the murder weapon, but also for any clues as to who had buried the girl there, but we found nothing.

You cannot imagine the trepidation with which I approached the dawning truth that I was facing the first murder investigation of my career. It was an appalling prospect, for which I felt totally unqualified. No amount of training, or of working in a junior capacity, can fully prepare one for the experience of being solely responsible for the investigation of a major crime, and I wondered whether I was up to it. Of course, the case was solved in the end: I should hardly be telling you this story if it recorded nothing but the first major disaster and the last case of a short and undistinguished career! I confided my fears to my wife, Beth, and she said, sagely enough, that I simply had to get on with it and that I was to stop being such a milksop.

My first duty, clearly, was to speak with the abbot. Our interview took place, the day after the discovery of the body, in the privacy of the abbot's office, an austere room sandwiched between the Abbot's Garden and the eastern arm of the cloister. No one could accuse the abbot of abusing his position to live in comfortable surroundings. There was a desk and a chair behind it for his use, and two chairs, without arms and barely upholstered, for visitors. The few pictures round the otherwise bare walls were of a religious nature. A small bookshelf was full, but of what I could not see: holy tomes, no doubt. The only ornament on the desk was a *memento mori* in best Rancé tradition. I did not beat about the bush.

'Father Abbot,' I began boldly, 'you will appreciate that the abbey is now in a very invidious position. It is quite clear to me, and to everybody else on our team, that one of your monks has been guilty of the murder of a young woman.'

'Inspector,' the abbot said, 'I appreciate your concern. I respect your reasoning. It is, however, quite beyond the bounds of possibility that any of us has perpetrated such an outrage, and I shall give you all the help I can in clearing our name.'

'You appreciate, of course, Father, that I cannot simply take your word for that? I shall have to interview every single monk, including yourself and the dead girl's brother, who, I concede, is hardly likely to be a suspect, and I should like to begin immediately.'

I discovered that in real life (so to speak) he had been a teacher of mathematics at a secondary school in Bristol before responding to 'the call'. I liked him, even though I should probably never have been able to call him a friend. He had been a monk for thirty years, abbot for three. (Monks were elected to fill the abbot's post for a seven year period. They then relapsed into ordinary monkhood. On the other hand, every monk had some responsibility, so no one need feel neglected or overlooked.) He shifted in his chair and said, after a short pause:

'If you should find that one of us is responsible, we shall not, naturally, put any obstacle in the path of your pursuit of justice, but may I ask you, in all earnestness, to spare us publicity? So far, I believe, if I make a correct deduction from the absence of reporters camping out at the abbey entrance, we have entirely escaped the attentions of the press, and I should like it to continue that way. I entreat you, Inspector, not to let this matter leak out. Even if, as I fully expect, you absolve all of us from the slightest complicity in whatever happened to Miss Fletcher, our reputation would be in tatters.'

'I quite understand, Father,' I said, 'and I shall do my level best, but you must realise that I may have to appeal to the public for assistance if our inquiries seem to be leading nowhere. Let us hope that we can clear the matter up without bringing it into the public realm. The only thing is, of course, that if our investigation should lead to an arrest and a court case, there is bound to be some publicity, but if you cooperate, I'm sure we can present the matter in a light favourable to the abbey: "Dastardly murder uncovered with the help of unworldly monks" – that sort of thing.'

The abbot's mobile face twisted into a sort of wry smile.

'Thank you for that. I suppose that's the best I can hope for. Where would you like to begin?'

'I'm sorry if this is awkward, but I should like to interview each monk through the rest of the afternoon, and perhaps into tomorrow morning, even though it cuts across chapel or other activities in the abbey. My sergeant and I will be perfectly comfortable in the Blue Parlour, if that suits you, and we shall be private there. So perhaps the best thing to do is to start with, say, the procurator, and then ask him to fetch the next man, and so on. Will that be all right?'

'Perfectly all right, Inspector. I'll ask the procurator to meet you in the Blue Parlour in a few minutes.'

Strictly speaking, I did not need my sergeant to be there, but two heads are better than one, particularly when one of them is mine, and how better could I involve Blundell in the investigation than by including him in the interviewing of – well, suspects, I suppose you'd have to call them?

The procurator appeared very shortly, and I did not find him a particularly prepossessing individual. He was a large man with thin lips and a rather morose face. His jowls sagged, and his nose and chin drooped, giving him the appearance of sliding downwards, but whether with the weight of responsibility or with the passage of years was impossible to tell. I should put him about mid-sixties, perhaps a little more. His name in religion was Ambrose (presumably to encourage him to emulate his namesake in piety, scholarship *and* administrative ability!). I started out as I meant to continue. That is to say, there were two questions to which I was most anxious to have the answers: most importantly, was every single monk present in chapel at eleven o'clock on that Saturday morning, the most likely time of Audrey's disappearance? and secondly, which of the monks knew she was in the building?

'Brother Procurator, Father Abbot will have explained to you the purpose of this little chat, and you will know that we are interviewing all the brothers in turn, from the top down.' Brother Ambrose took in good part my attempt at a small joke. 'Would you just explain to me the seating in chapel?'

'Certainly, Inspector,' he said, in a very smooth, cultured voice. 'We sit on opposite sides of the choir, that is, the top part of the chapel, where the seating faces across the building instead of up the way.'

'Do you always occupy the same seats?'

'Yes.'

'And if any of the brothers are absent?'

'The gap remains unfilled. We don't shuffle up, if that's what you mean.'

'And if several are missing from one side of the chapel and none from the other?'

'Makes no difference.'

'I see. So there are nine of you on each side of the choir, facing each other. Would you necessarily notice if anyone were missing?'

The bursar thought for a minute.

'Well,' he said cautiously, 'sometimes for a short office, I might not look up or notice who was on the opposite side. We are enjoined to keep custody of the eyes, you know, so we generally concentrate on our breviaries or *libri usuales*. But I should have thought it unusual for no one to notice a gap on the opposite side, if that's what you're driving at.'

That was exactly what I was driving at, but I didn't say so.

'And what about your immediate neighbours?'

'Oh, there's no doubt I should notice a gap there. You see, we Gilbertines observe the custom of acknowledging our neighbours at the start and end of each office. We don't talk much – such a distraction – but we are all brothers, and it is good to externalise that fact. So at the beginning and end of the offices, we bow briefly to the person on each side of us; or perhaps just give a quick nod of the head. And even I, old dotard that I am, would notice if I were bowing to an empty seat!'

'Quite so, Brother. You have made matters admirably clear. Tell me now, if you would, who would know that Brother Jude's sister Audrey was visiting the abbey that morning?'

'Father Abbot, of course, and the porter detailed to admit her if she was expected. That was probably Brother Jude anyway. That's all.'

'And who might have seen her here?'

'Now you're asking! I shouldn't have thought anybody, except Brother Jude. All of us would be otherwise occupied. And in any case we walk with our eyes downcast: we don't make a habit of peering about for strangers!'

'No, no, of course not. But *could* anyone else have seen her?'

'Well, I suppose so. In theory it's certainly possible.'

'Who, for example?'

'Well, say a brother cleaning the gate-house, or the guest-master coming out of the guest wing. That's about all though, I should have thought.'

I shall spare you an account of all the interviews the sergeant and I conducted that afternoon and the following morning. Sometimes I asked the questions, sometimes Blundell did. Occasionally we chipped in together. It was all very civilised. The monks included young men – one reminded me of the sacred historian's description of David in the first *Book of Samuel*: 'Now he was ruddy, and withal of a beautiful countenance, and goodly to look to' – and old men, the lively and the reticent, the raw-boned and the lithe, the portly and the lean. Some had joined the community straight from school or college, some had pursued careers 'in the world' first, but I was impressed with the courtesy, patience and good-humour that characterised them all. There was not a curmudgeon amongst them, whatever the physical appearances. The only monk we did not interview was Brother Denis, who was in the infirmary. As he was ninety-four years old, in very poor health, not quite *compos mentis* and virtually blind to boot, I just could not see him gambolling about the abbey after a young girl, stabbing her, carrying the body out to the cemetery, digging a grave and burying the corpse, and then returning unnoticed to his bed. No, I felt justified in giving him a miss, although I did question the policemen who had searched the infirmary and got them to confirm that an aged monk was indeed sick in bed. (They opined that, from his looks, the patient might just reach the infirmary bathroom, two yards away, on his own but would certainly not have the strength to make his way back without assistance!)

Finally we went through the same questions with the abbot. The upshot of this lengthy process was precisely zilch. Well, almost zilch. We established, beyond a peradventure and to our entire satisfaction, that every single monk, with the sole exception of Brother Denis, attended sext that Saturday morning: the entire community was in the chapel from the moment when Audrey made her way to the front-door to the end of the office. A cast-iron alibi. Oh, hell. And not a single monk, with the exceptions of Brother Jude, naturally, and Brother Simon who had admitted her because he happened to be passing the gate-house and heard the knocker, admitted having seen her in the flesh. What a case for my first one: was ever a young inspector so unfortunately placed?

Then there was a totally unexpected development, about which I shall now tell you. I hoped that it spelt my salvation – a way out of the maze in which I found myself - but as it turned out, it mired me even further.

Five

Before I tell you in detail what that extraordinary event was, I must just give you the gist of the discussion that my sergeant and I had at this point, lest you think us complete numbskulls without the ability to weigh the implications of what had already taken place. (They were weighed, but it was we who were found wanting.)

When we had concluded interviewing the monks and were satisfied that nothing more could usefully be accomplished in that line, we bade goodbye to the abbot, who was the last to attend our inquisition, and returned to the station in, as you may imagine, pensive mood. We decided that lunch in a public house was indicated, and we repaired to the Warwickshire Oak, on foot, to imbibe and to refresh the inner man. After a modest meal of chicken and chips and apple and blackberry tart, we embarked on our serious discussion. I began, as I have done ever since, by asking the sergeant what he thought. This is not, to set your suspicious mind at rest, an abdication of my responsibility as investigator-in-chief; it is rather an attempt to imbue my assistant with a sense of his value to the investigation and to encourage him to come to conclusions of his own, which might, of course, be different from my own, but which could nevertheless be more to the point. Honest.

'Well, Sergeant, what are your thoughts?'

'Well, Sir, we seem to have comprehensively established an unbreakable alibi for every single inmate of the abbey, unless ... '

'Yes? "Unless"?'

' ... they are all acting in concert, and I really don't think that's likely.'

'No, nor do I. Go on.'

'But the pathologist also knocked on the head any idea we might have had of motive.'

'How do you mean?'

'Well, here we have eighteen men cooped up together without sight of a female from one year's end to the next. However many knots they tie in their willies, they are going to be tantalised by urges some time or other – or I'm barking up a very strange tree. There can surely be only one motive for the murder of an attractive young woman in a monastery. And yet the pathologist rules out sexual assault. I just don't get it. Why go the trouble of murdering someone and then get nothing out of it?'

'OK. We've been working on the assumption that one of the monks is responsible for Audrey's death. Could anyone else have had access to the monastery or the cemetery?'

'Not really, I should have thought. For one thing, the last sighting of her was in the monastery gatehouse: if she had emerged into the outside world at all, she would have been seen by her sister ten minutes later. If she was seen by a passing motorist, for example, and bumped off, why – and how – was she buried in the abbey cemetery? For another, the cemetery is practically accessible only from within the monastery. I mean, I suppose someone could climb over fences and walls, but with a body that wouldn't be easy, and in any case there's no evidence for it. There just wasn't time for all that, between Audrey's disappearance and the monks coming out of chapel after sext. I'm flummoxed.'

'So am I, Sergeant, so am I. And what do you make of burying the body in the abbey cemetery?'

'Well, Sir, I've thought about that, and the only thing I could up with was a feminist gesture of contempt for monastic celibacy. Not very a clever one, though, is it?'

'Could it have been some faint attempt to give the girl decent burial in consecrated ground: a sort of gesture of repentance?'

'Possibly, Sir, but I don't think either explanation sheds much light on the problem, if I may say so.'

'Incidentally, in case you're wondering, there have been two guests at the abbey this week: monks from Mount St Bernard's Abbey, but they were definitely out all that Saturday visiting some monastery in Worcestershire. I checked. So we seem to be at an impasse, as our French friends have it, or, in plain English, in a cul-de-sac. No way forward at all.'

Blundell then brought up the business of the scuffle in Church Street and wondered whether further investigation would open up new avenues for us. I thought not, since uniform had seemingly discovered all there was to discover. Both of us agreed that the girl seen on the ground in the Warwick street was probably just dazed, or in any case only slightly injured, and just got up and walked home. A storm in a tea-cup.

It was a week after this conversation that I had a phone-call from the abbot asking us to go over as soon as possible. He sounded agitated. We fixed a time and drove up to Our Lady of the Snows, on an overcast but warm day, a slight drizzle in the air. We were intrigued to know what could have prompted the abbot to call us back after our fruitless interviews of the week before. Had one of the monks confessed? Were the monks prepared to name a name? Had another body appeared?

'I'm glad you could make it so promptly, Inspector. I really need advice!'

'Yes, Father, we're only too happy to help if we can, as you know. What seems to be the problem?'

'Earlier this morning there was a phone-call. It was taken by Brother Augustine and put through to me in my office. He says it was definitely from a public phone-box, because he heard the money drop as the caller pushed button A. The voice on the other end of the line was male, not disguised in any way, I should say, and without any detectable regional accent. I certainly didn't recognise the voice as belonging to anyone I know.'

'Yes, Father,' I said encouragingly. 'What did this man have to say?'

'That's the extraordinary thing! I still can't make sense of it.'

'But what did he say?'

'You'll understand that I can't give you a word for word account of our conversation. I was taken by surprise, and it was as much as I could do to focus on the gist of what he was saying.'

'Yes, yes, Father, we take that for granted. Please' – PLEASE! – 'go on: what did he say?'

'First of all, he wanted reassurance that it was definitely the abbot he was speaking to: nobody else would do. Then he said that he knew for a certainty which of the monks had murdered Audrey Fletcher, and that he had proof. If he were not to go to the police with the evidence, we had to - But I still can't believe it!'

'What do you have to do?' I said, by this time getting just a tiny bit exasperated, even though I sympathised with the abbot's shock or stupefaction or incredulity or whatever was the emotion under which he was labouring.

'We have to sell the Hermann manuscript and give the proceeds to a named charity.'

This meant very little to us two sinners, so I begged to be enlightened. The abbot took a little time to become properly coherent, and I reproduce the general tenor of his hesitant discourse in an edited version, so that you don't have to endure the loopings and twistings that Blundell and I did. The Hermann manuscript was a very valuable item in the abbey's treasury – the *only* valuable item – which had belonged to the abbey since the Reformation, and to the order since the very beginning. Very few people knew of its existence, probably not even all the monks. The manuscript had to be offered for sale at public auction, in London, presumably so that the best price was achieved. The charity named was Christians for Justice, and the caller would make it his business to contact the charity within a month of the auction to verify that it had received the full proceeds of the sale. At this point I asked the abbot what guarantee the caller had given that this charitable gesture would satisfy him.

'He said that once he was satisfied the price realised by the manuscript had been sent in full to Christians for Justice, he would send me, by post, the murder weapon and two other items of proof: a fragment of monastic habit with blood on it and a few male hairs that had been clutched in the girl's hand. If we did not cooperate, these three items would be sent to the police.'

'And how long did he give you to comply?'

'Three months. Auctioneers Chapman and Thomas were holding a sale of early books and incunabula in September, and he expected the Hermann manuscript to be included.'

'Did you challenge him on guarantees?'

'I did. All he said was, that if we kept faith with the poor, he would keep faith with us.'

'And who else have you told of this conversation?'

'Oh, no one. You are the first.'

'Before we go any further, I'd like to see this manuscript, if I may. I feel I'm wandering in the dark.'

'Certainly, although I must tell you that you are extraordinarily privileged, since few people have ever set eyes on it. It's not exactly under lock and key, and we could never afford realistic insurance, so it's sort of kept hidden. You'll see what I mean, and to our way of thinking, the fewer people that know about it, the better. However, let's go and have a look at it. And we shall need the assistance of Brother Pragmatius, the librarian.'

'Pragmatius'? Good heavens!

The abbot led the way round the cloisters to the library, where we gathered Brother – er – Pragmatius to our bosom, and then the four of us proceeded to the scriptorium. This was a room about twenty feet by eighteen situated to the north of the refectory and having windows only to the north and west. The furniture consisted of four copying-desks, with stools, and cupboards, nothing else. However, the wooden floor and exposed ceiling beams gave the space a warm and gracious, if slightly heavy, appearance.

'This is where the monks copied manuscripts in the early days of the monastery, before printed books became available,' explained the abbot.

'Do you mean to say that this room hasn't been used since?' I asked in disbelief.

'Oh, no,' the abbot hurriedly answered, 'it's used by any monk who has an interest in reproducing mediaeval manuscripts. We do produce a few manuscripts now and again, whenever we have with us a monk sufficiently skilled in the art, and we present them to illustrious guests as gifts. The cupboards contain all that is necessary: parchment, instruments for pricking the parchment, styluses and quills and even reeds, inks, erasing knives, and so forth, as well as examples of mediaeval art for beginners to copy from. In the library we have some treatises on the different styles and ages of notation. All very professional, really.'

'I see,' I said. 'And the Hermann manuscript?'

The librarian went to one of the cupboards, opened the outer doors and bent down to the bottom drawer. He fished out a wooden box, which he proceeded to open with a key hanging from his waist. What he produced from the box had us gawping in amazement: a simply exquisite illuminated manuscript. Let me try to describe it more fully for you, although I cannot hope to recreate our own first emotion of amazement and admiration. The binding was leather on board, about A4 size, with four corner bosses and a boss in the centre carrying the single initial M (for Maria, I supposed). The four folios contained within the binding were parchment. Each page had a rich floral border, inside which were three or four lines of music and text, set round an illustration from the life of the Virgin Mary. The first A of the text was exotically worked and contained within it an annunciation scene. I asked the librarian to explain a bit more what we were looking at.

'Well, I'm no expert, unfortunately,' he said by way of introduction. Pragmatius was thin and stooped, with thinning hair but bushy eyebrows. I should put him in his forties. Clearly a cultivated man. 'I'm told that the style of notation and of the art-work can be dated to the middle of the eleventh century, and that the parchment is consistent with this. The text is of the Marian anthem or antiphon – it is variously termed – *Alma Redemptoris Mater*, for centuries and even now sung at Sunday Compline in Christmastide. Because the manuscript is in pristine condition – no finger marks or wax stains, that sort of thing – it is thought to have been intended as a presentation-copy to some grandee, secular or ecclesiastical, and that it has never, or rarely, been used in worship.'

'And how does it get its name, the "Hermann Manuscript"?' I asked.

'Ah, well, that's very interesting, you know,' and I could almost see the librarian debating within himself about how much detail to burden us with.

'It's technical listing in international inventories is GB – OS An 7, and any other name is only colloquial. Hermann was a Benedictine monk who died in 1054 at the early age of forty-one, but he stands out from his contemporaries for one peculiarity: he was hopelessly crippled. Modern medicine has suggested that he suffered from a cleft palate, cerebral palsy and spina bifida, all at once. He couldn't talk properly, and he couldn't move unaided; he could hardly sit up on his own. He was nobly born – his father was a count, I believe – and he was sent, at the age of seven – seven! – to the Benedictine monastery on the island of Reichenau in Lake Constance. There he lived, and there he died. But the range of his learning and skills was prodigious and soon made him a legendary figure in Europe: he was a linguist, a poet, an astronomer and mathematician, a historian and a musician, equally adept in theory and in practice in all these areas. His early death was a sad loss to European culture. One of his achievements was composing two Marian hymns, the *Salve Regina*, still greatly loved amongst Catholics, and the *Alma Redemptoris Mater*. What we have here is possibly the original committal of this latter hymn to parchment, in celebration of that glorious work. In parts, possibly even in its totality, it could be by Hermann himself: text, plainchant and execution of the manuscript! As you can appreciate, this makes it a European treasure of enormous worth.'

Blundell and I were, naturally, impressed.

'Is he a saint?' Blundell asked.

'No, not exactly, but his Christian virtues, not least courage in overriding his disabilities, meant that he was beatified in the nineteenth century – that's a major step towards sainthood - and that Christians could do worse than imitate him.'

'And how did it come into possession of Our Lady of the Snows?' This was an obvious question, I know, but I couldn't wait for the librarian to tell us in his own time!

'I can tell you that,' the abbot piped up. 'When our Founder of blessed memory, Gilbert of Sempringham, came to draw up a rule for his order, he thought first of all of the Benedictines – as you know, he eventually decided in favour of the particular brand of Benedictinism known as Cistercians - and with this in mind he travelled to one of the most famous Benedictine monasteries of his day, Reichenau, in Germany. Here he was well received, and as a gift to the new order-in-the-making, the abbot of Reichenau handed over the Hermann manuscript. It was certainly a rare gift; an extraordinary gift. It was housed first, discreetly, at Sempringham, but in the uncertain times of Henry VIII's reign, it was secretly transferred to Our Lady of the Snows for safer keeping. It turned out to be a very wise move, since the manuscript has escaped the depredations of the ungodly ever since.'

The librarian then came in with what was, for him, an obvious question.

'Father Abbot,' he said, 'why are we talking about the Hermann manuscript? Why are you showing it to these gentlemen, if I may ask?'

The abbot proceeded to outline the telephone conversation he had had earlier that morning, and it brought us all back to earth. How was the abbey to respond to the caller's demand? The abbot looked to me, significantly.

'Look, Father,' I said, 'I shall need to think about it, although I don't imagine the police would have any advice to give you, one way or the other. Perhaps a first step is for you to formulate some official abbey decision, perhaps in consultation with your monks, and then you and I can have a chat. How would that do?'

As this suggestion relieved the abbot of making any personal decision there and then, I could see that it was accepted with gratitude.

'I shall summon a full convocation of the brothers,' he said, 'and I shall get back to you in a day or two: Monday, perhaps?'

I concurred, and Blundell and I left the monastery full of theories and surmises. I also realised that I should need to go back to Miss Elspeth Fletcher with an account of this latest development, but I shall tell you about that in a minute.

Despite his parting words, it was the following day, not Monday, that the abbot phoned me again.

'Inspector,' he said, 'we're all agreed that we want everything to be above board and open to inspection, to obviate the slightest hint of suspicion. Would you be kind enough to attend our chapter meeting as an observer? It will take place tomorrow, at twelve noon, after the usual Sunday High Mass. We should be very pleased for your attendance, and perhaps you would do us the honour of staying on for lunch afterwards, you and your sergeant.'

I did not feel I could very well turn this invitation down, not only because it was part of the case as it unfolded, but also because I was curious to know how the monks would respond to a threat from a blackmailer. The following day, therefore, found Blundell and me in our Sunday best, sitting in the chapter-house of Our Lady of the Snows along with seventeen cowled monks all looking very serious. The chapter house, or *capitulum*, as in most monastic establishments, as I understand it, was entered from the cloister. At Our Lady of the Snows, it was a handsome if austere building, octagonal, with a vault supported on a central pillar. Blind arcades ran round the walls, and all the seats, twenty-four in all, were simple benches, apart from the seats provided for the abbot and his two senior monks, which were a triple sedilia in a triple arch. On this occasion, the abbot was assisted by Brothers Ambrose (procurator) and Heribert (guest-master). The chapter-house was cool in the summer warmth, but I wondered how cosy it would be in mid-winter.

The abbot began with a short prayer to the Holy Ghost. Then he welcomed us two, handsomely I thought, and then the meeting proper began.

'Brothers,' the abbot said, 'let me just remind you all that we are here to discuss a very grave situation in which the abbey unexpectedly finds itself. I wish you to know from the outset that I do not feel it either possible or seemly for me to take a decision on my own, and I therefore propose that we take a vote at the end of the chapter, and that that decisions holds. Is everyone agreed?'

All were, if a silent nod of heads was anything to go by. I should perhaps add that, immediately after the opening prayer, all the monks had slid their cowls back over their heads, so that they looked slightly more human.

'Let me put before you the course of action that is demanded of us. Most of you will know of the existence of a valuable mediaeval manuscript in the abbey's possession. It is the only thing of value in the place – except for our immortal souls, of course,' he added with a slight chuckle. 'We are asked to put this manuscript up for sale at public auction, within the next three months, and then to donate the entire proceeds to the charity called Christians for Justice. Thereafter, our' – with a noticeable hesitation – 'blackmailer, having checked with the charity, will hand over to us the incriminating evidence he claims to have. Now, has anybody any thoughts?'

For a moment nobody stirred. Then a tentative hand was partially raised.

'Yes, Bernard?'

'Father Abbot, how can we know that this isn't a hoax? Perhaps it's a confidence trick, and the blackmailer has no evidence whatever. In fact, if we're all innocent, I don't see how he can have any evidence.'

'Good question. How would anybody like to answer that?'

'The thing is, Bernard,' a voice said, 'can we take the risk? What if he does go the press and publicises his accusations? What then?' The speaker was a rough-hewn individual, broad-shouldered and granite-featured. He spoke softly, but his voice was redolent of aristocratic drawing-rooms and university libraries.

'We laugh at him, Reginald. We proclaim our innocence to the world!'

Another voice struck in: Brother Thomas, it turned out to be.

'That's all very well, Bernard, but you know what people are, ever ready to believe the worst of us monks. The accusation would stick, I fear, in defiance of all reason.'

'And what if it does, Thomas?' asked another.

'I'm afraid it would be a great scandal, however baseless, for our own abbey and for the wider church,' said Thomas.

'Father Abbot,' chimed in another voice.

'Yes, Matthias?' This monk, one of the youngest there, I should say, was not afraid to voice his opinion in front of his much older brethren. I admired him for the confidence and poise with which he spoke.

'Has the abbey the right to sell an heirloom? It was given to our forebears by the mother house, not for us to flog at the first

54

opportunity, but to safeguard, generation after generation, as a sacred treasure. Do we not owe an allegiance to the mother house, even though it is no more? It's our history that it is proposed we part with, and I think European monasticism would in years to come scorn our short-termism and our timid response to threats.'

'That's all very well,' said Ambrose – whom I knew, of course, from previous acquaintance – 'but have we no duty to the poor? What's the use of hanging on to a manuscript that few of us ever bother with, when our brothers and sisters in the world are suffering for want of justice?'

'We are poor people,' answered Brother Matthias, 'and our effectiveness depends not on scattering charity left, right and centre, but in purposeful prayer. Let others see to practical needs: our role is spiritual, and we should not be sidetracked by worldly considerations.'

'On the other hand,' Brother Pragmatius said, 'Ambrose is right to point out that now, unexpectedly, we have a golden opportunity to practise charity. This doesn't in any way deny the usefulness of our prayers, but it adds another dimension to them.'

'Can I say something, Father?' This, we discovered, was Brother Anselm, who had particular charge of the growing of the abbey's vegetables. I should say that he would be more comfortable with a spade in his hand than in speaking in public or conning learned tomes, but I may be doing him an injustice. His intervention in the discussion was certainly lucid and to the point.

'Of course, Anselm, go ahead.'

'Could we not turn our necessity, if that's what it becomes, to our advantage? We could and should trumpet our sale of the manuscript as a selfless gesture of solidarity with the poor. People would then admire the abbey for its gesture. There is no requirement, as I understand the matter, requiring us to tell the world that we are yielding to blackmail!'

'Should we not copy the example of our holy father the pope?' This was Brother Florentius. How do monks live with such names? And who confers them on twentieth-century people?

'How do you mean, Florentius?' said the abbot, when the monk paused.

'The Vatican is stuffed full of treasures, but the pope doesn't sell them all off!'

'No,' said another voice, 'but perhaps he should do!'

'Let us not wrangle,' the abbot hastily intervened. 'Other points of view, please?'

Brother Cedd asked permission to speak.

'Father, this situation has forced us to consider the best use of our only treasure. Is hiding it in a drawer the very best way of using it? I'm not agreeing with the blackmailer, that we should sell it off, but perhaps we should ask whether we could not make its beauty more widely known? Make a small charge for people to view it, for example?'

'The trouble with that is, Cedd,' said Brother Ambrose, 'we'd be involving ourselves in insurance premiums and much more expensive security measures – a whole heap more trouble and expense.'

'Then,' said Cedd boldly, 'I propose we sell it!'

'May I say something?' This was Brother Sebastian. 'If we sell the manuscript, are we not tacitly admitting amongst ourselves that there is truth in the accusation that one of us is a murderer?'

And so the debate wound on. I do not repeat the rest of it, because there was much repetition and meandering, and I believe I have recorded for you the main points that arose. Nearly everybody spoke at some stage, I think. Finally the abbot proposed a vote.

'Brothers, I think everybody who wishes has had a say. May I comment that I am very grateful for the fraternal and even mood of this gathering. We are faced with a difficult choice, and I believe it right that we attempt to come to a decision together. The vote will be simply on the proposition, Do we sell the manuscript or not? Yes or no. I hope that those who find themselves in the minority after the vote will not hold it against their brethren: that would be to contravene the injunction to exercise charity at all times. I am sure that all our votes will be the expression of sincere sentiment and conviction.'

Before so solemn a moment, he paused and briefly bowed his tonsured head. He was clearly not relieved of all sense of responsibility for the vote that was about to be taken. I felt for him at this difficult time. If I had followed the discussion accurately, there were two major concerns on each side of the issue. On the one hand, to sell the Hermann manuscript was firstly to cave in to threats and secondly to misuse the abbey's patrimony. On the other hand, to keep the manuscript was firstly to deny the poor what could be of enormous help to them and secondly to expose the abbey to serious risk of scandal. A difficult one. I wondered what I myself should decide in the circumstances.

'Brothers, please raise your hand clearly if you believe that the abbey should sell the Hermann manuscript.'

Seven hands went up, including his own.

'And if you believe that the abbey should not sell the Hermann manuscript, please raise your hand clearly now.'

Six hands were raised, including, I noticed, that of Brother Jude, even though he had not felt strongly enough about the matter to speak during the deliberations.

'And if you deliberately abstain from committing yourself, please raise your hand now.'

Four hands went up.

'Thank you. The abbey is thereby committed to putting the Hermann manuscript up for sale by public auction. The proceeds will be donated entirely to the charity named by our mysterious caller. Thank you, brothers. Let us say the *Salve, Regina* together' – what else could he have suggested in the circumstances, I asked myself! – 'and proceed to lunch.'

Because of the abbot's invitation to attend the chapter meeting, it was Sunday evening before I was able to return to Warwick to keep an appointment I had made with Elspeth Fletcher. I felt that she ought to be told of the blackmail call, but by the time I got round to doing so, the chapter at which a decision to sell the Hermann manuscript had been made had taken place: double the news, if you like. So I went along to Miss Fletcher's flat and found her in a depressed state. She told me that she was finding it very difficult to come to terms with her sister's death and that her brother was no use to her in her mourning because he was invisible and effectively out of contact. I reassured her that we were doing all we could to identify her sister's killer and that we had some hopes of achieving this if the blackmailer stood by his undertaking to hand over evidence. As we talked, her constraint eased, and she confessed that identifying the monk responsible was no longer an item on her agenda.

'Why is that?' I asked, with genuine curiosity.

'Because it can't have been one of the monks,' she answered. 'You've proved to me that all the monks, apart from one in the infirmary, were in the chapel at the time Audrey disappeared. And I can also understand that none of the monks had the slightest motive for killing her. Audrey's dead, that's the gross fact, and I am half reconciled to never knowing who was responsible. I know you are doing your best, and I'm grateful, but if you don't succeed, I shan't worry.'

I accepted this asseveration in the spirit of respect (for the police) and resignation (to her circumstances) in which I think it was intended.

'Well, Miss Fletcher, I shall come back to you if we should hear from the blackmailer again. In the meantime, thank you so much for your understanding.'

We parted on, I think, amiable terms, given the circumstances.

Six

Another week passed before I again heard from the monastery. It was, of course, the abbot.

'Inspector,' the voice said diffidently, 'Brother Ambrose has contacted the auction rooms in London named by our, er, correspondent, but I wonder whether I might ask a favour of you?'

'By all means,' I said graciously, 'only too happy to oblige if I can.' Always the magnanimous volunteer, that's me.

'The auction house will not collect the Hermann manuscript, except at prohibitive cost, and it would be doing us an enormous favour if you could see your way to conveying the, er, goods to Hammersmith. I'm sure we should be allowed modest expenses incurred in our transaction.'

'It will be a pleasure,' I said truthfully.

'But will your superintendent allow you to do so, Inspector?'

'I am due some time off. So, I think, is my sergeant. We shall be more than happy to continue our involvement in your troubles. I am far from forgetting that there is an outstanding crime to be solved, and I am keen to exonerate all your members' – probably quite the wrong word – 'if possible.'

It fell out, therefore, that Blundell and I travelled up to the London with the Hermann manuscript cunningly disguised in a brown paper bag and handed it over to Chapman and Thomas, Auctioneers, whose insurance would take care of it from then on. In due course a catalogue was produced, which the abbot showed me, and the plainsong manuscript showed up to full advantage on two pages devoted to it alone. Because it was almost unknown, except to a few keen collectors, the auctioneers had taken the precaution of sketching in its history, describing it in full, and saying something adulatory and expansive about Hermann the Cripple. The spread was certainly impressive. I was therefore all agog to attend the auction itself. I also convinced myself that attendance was obligatory, since I might pick up some clue as to the identity of the blackmailer, whom I took also to be the murderer. We policemen never rest. Since the abbey was not going to be represented, as the abbot could justify neither the time nor the expense in the services of what was essentially a secular transaction, I promised to phone through the sale figure – which, of course, presumed there would be someone on the other end of the line to receive my call!

I was half-minded – that is to say, the idea flickered for one millisecond through my brain – to bid for the manuscript myself and then donate it back to the monastery, but I quickly realised that my modest salary was unlikely to stretch that far and that in any case I had no such duty, however elastic one's definition of Christian charity. And as for what Beth would say: I dared not imagine it!

The great day arrived, and Blundell and I drove up to London. We had not needed, naturally, to attend the preview, having been privileged to examine the Hermann manuscript at close quarters in its own surroundings. We parked in a side-street – London was not quite so crowded in those days as it is today – and made our way into the auction-room. Others were arriving, and from their appearance and that of their clothing, it was an international gathering. If the blackmailer were in attendance, what would he look like? Do crooks look crooked? How could I identify him amongst the scores of people present? And if I did, should I then accost him and arrest him? Policemen, however hard-headed, are not immune to fantasy, you know.

The room was large and crowded with furniture. The sale of manuscripts was not scheduled to begin before mid-afternoon. Those attending the auction sat on sofas and in arm-chairs, or perched on the edges of tables and Victorian commodes, many of them with catalogues in their hands or pieces of paper on which they had (presumably) marked the numbers of the lots in which they were interested. There was a constant to'ing and fro'ing as the auctioneer's assistants moved round the room, from item to item, and potential purchasers changed their position to ensure that the auctioneer could see their discreet gestures indicating a willingness to bid. And so the bidding continued through the morning as the auctioneer balanced his duty to the vendors – ensuring that all bidders had ample opportunity to voice their offers - with his duty to complete the sale in one day without undue tedium. There was an hour's break for lunch, after which the last of the furniture was disposed of: dining-room tables, chairs that matched or did not match, tall-boys, display cabinets, and so on. By three o'clock the auctioneer was ready to turn his attention to the series of manuscripts and incunabula that would take us through to the five o'clock finish. Virtually all the manuscripts were mediaeval, on vellum and parchment, of a legal, theological, biblical, philosophical and historical nature, single folios or entire volumes.

The auctioneer was a young man, blonde, with a large wart on his chin and a face that I should describe as determined. This was clearly not his first auction, as he swept from lot to lot with the adroitness of an experienced practitioner. I imagined his being the son of the auction-house, brought up to the business with his mother's milk, his name Chapman or Thomas, probably – unless, of course, he'd married the *daughter* of the house and his name was Dent or Tishbold. Idle speculations as I waited for the Hermann manuscript to come up. Eventually it did, held aloft by a sleek assistant in white gloves, firstly in its polished box, then in its nakedness, folio by folio. A movement in the room suggested, to me at any rate, that this item was the star of the show. I observed people, too far from the scene of the action to have a clear view but anxious to savour the excitement of the moment, staring at the illustration of the first page of the manuscript in their catalogues, with its glorious colours, its dexterous art-work, the unusual fashion of the plainchant notes ascending and descending in, to the untutored eye random, waves, and the pristine condition of the whole.

'And now, Ladies and Gentlemen, a very rare manuscript, GB – OS An 7, known to us layfolk as the Hermann Manuscript. The vendors make no claim as to its authenticity, but it is thought by some to be the original work of the eleventh-century polymath Hermann the Cripple, or Hermann of Reichenau, and to owe its present immaculate condition to having had effectively only two careful owners all its life. The music sets Hermann's words to a Gregorian chant, and the illumination is skilful almost beyond belief. Ladies and Gentlemen, who will give me £2000 for it? £1000? ... Yes, Sir, in the corner. Any advance? £1250, the lady in the front row. £1500, anyone? ... Yes, Sir, on my right. £1750 in front of me.'

The bidding mounted, and it became clear after £5000 that there were two serious contenders left, both men, one I should say British, the other continental, perhaps German. The sums proposed crept up steadily in units of £250, until the sum of £11,500 was reached. This was an enormous figure, considering that the average price of houses at that time was, I should have thought, less than £2000, and I rejoiced that Christians for Justice would benefit so hugely. The foreign gentleman hesitated. The auctioneer gave an extra few seconds, but he finally brought his hammer down at £11,500: 'Gone to the gentleman on my left! A very happy purchase, if I may say so, Sir,' as he swept on to the next lot.

Blundell and I made our way out, as did quite a few others, marvelling that four pages of parchment could command such a figure. We stopped at a phone-box to leave a message for the abbot, and drove back to Warwickshire, pausing on the way for a bite to eat to round off our interesting journey. It would now be up to Father Abbot and Brother Ambrose to conclude the rest of the business, and I did not expect to be further involved. My expectation was not met. This case threw up the most extraordinary developments!

The latest twist came about in this way. The monks in chapter (I gathered) thought that it would be good to celebrate publicly the donation of the proceeds to the proposed charity, and to do so, it was thought suitable to hold a service in the monastery chapel at which a rendering of the *Alma Mater Redemptoris* would be given pride of place. The service would be open to the public, but entry would be by (free) ticket only, because of restrictions of space. A choir from Mount St Bernard's Abbey in Leicestershire, a Cistercian foundation which had assumed the role of Mother House to Our Lady of the Snows, were to join with the monks of the latter establishment to sing the anthem at the beginning and at the close of a service of thanksgiving, which would also include a plainsong setting of the Te Deum. After the service, refreshments would be offered in the refectory. As guest of honour, the abbey was inviting the purchaser of the Hermann manuscript, one Professor Theobald Dodsworth, an acknowledged expert in the field, and he was to say a few words at the reception. To my delight, Blundell and I received an invitation.

The day chosen was a Sunday a few weeks after the auction. Some local dignitaries had been invited (for example, the Mayor of Warwick and the Provost of Coventry Cathedral, in whose [Anglican] diocese we were); likewise the press both local and national; and of course a representative of Christians for Justice. It was the first Sunday in October, and the weather could not have been more gracious. The monastery glittered in the autumnal sun; the colours of the trees were spectacular, with the fiery reds, and the golden browns, and the brilliant yellows, and the still lush greens, spattered with the silver of the leaf-shedding birches. Perhaps, as St Theresa of Lisieux might have said, Our Lady had micromanaged the weather to suit the pomp and circumstance of the occasion. The cars drew up until the drive and forecourt of the monastery were full; they then spilled out on to the road. I estimated the crowd at over a hundred: such as the abbey had never probably witnessed before, and a challenge to the bursar to accommodate everyone comfortably in the chapel, and afterwards in the refectory.

The service proceeded without mishap. To many present, the sequence of psalms, prayers and readings, all in Latin, must have seemed a little strange, but there was no doubting the enthusiasm of the monks or the solemnity of the gathering. The monks from St Bernard's Abbey and their hosts from Our Lady of the Snows were squeezed into the choir at the top of the chapel, while the congregation sat in the pews and on extra chairs brought in for the occasion. The abbot of Our Lady of the Snows presided, and his rich baritone resounded round the building. As Blundell and I had no call to regard ourselves as in anyway favoured over the rest of the guests, we took our place where we could, and what we lacked in close range we made up for in broad view. Even from our vantage point near the back of the chapel, the *Alma Redemptoris Mater*, issuing from the mouths of a score and more of monks, had a touching poignancy. I hope Hermann on his gilded cloud was happy with the result.

After the service, the abbot and the monks led the way to the refectory for a creditable spread of canapés produced by the Our Lady of the Snows' monks, complete with home made breads, cheeses and honeys. As the food disappeared, the abbot called for silence and announced that Professor Dodsworth would say a few words to mark the occasion. A ripple of applause greeted this announcement.

'Ladies and Gentlemen,' the professor said, standing near the top table in full view of the assembled guests. He did not really fit the traditional caricature. He was a dapper little man, with sensitive hands, a delicate face, and a thin voice; elderly, but upright and spry, with a good head of hair, a moustache but no beard, spectacles on a cord round his neck. He was able to command the assembly's attention without effort. 'Ladies and Gentlemen, it gives me the greatest pleasure to be here tonight and to respond to the abbot's invitation to say a few words. You may be wondering what is my particular interest in the Hermann manuscript, and I shall now tell you. Many years ago, when I was an undergraduate, I was given an assignment on Hermannus Constrictus, as I knew him then, and I was fascinated by his life and his work. As part of that assignment, I asked the then abbot of Our Lady of the Snows, Father Walter, if I could view the Hermann manuscript. He could not have been more helpful. I was given access to the manuscript in the scriptorium' – and the professor gestured vaguely in the direction of the cloisters – 'and allowed to study it for an afternoon and to make a copy of it – of the text and music, I should say: the illumination was a little beyond me!' A polite ripple of laughter greeted this admission. 'I handled it with a sense of deep emotion, remembering the author's tragic life and immovable good-humour and famed generosity. That afternoon lived on in my memory, and I shall not disguise from you that I dreamt of one day owning that incredibly eloquent manuscript. It is now my pride, and I am touched beyond description that the monks of Our Lady of the Snows have seen fit to donate the entire proceeds of its sale to charity. Blessed Hermann must be overjoyed that his work is now to benefit so many nine hundred years after his untimely death.' Loud applause greeted this short speech, and there was the incipient murmur of resumed conversation round the refectory.

However, the abbot stepped forward again, briskly, and invited the representative of Christians for Justice to join him. He said it gave him the greatest pleasure to make a substantial donation, on behalf of the abbey, to so worthy a cause. The representative, a middle-aged woman of smart appearance, wearing tortoiseshell spectacles and a prim floral hat, was very gracious in her acceptance of the cheque, and there was much applause after she had uttered a few words of thanks, which seemed to this listener to match in sincerity the size of the cheque (as well it might).

I happened to be standing next to Brother Pragmatius shortly after this, when the professor came over to him, rubbing his hands, with a roguish smile on his gentle face.

'Ah, Brother,' he said, 'I understand you rehearsed the monks in tonight's singing. Excellent, excellent. I thoroughly enjoyed it.'

It was obvious that the professor had something to add, so Brother Pragmatius waited.

'I was very disappointed, however, that you didn't manage the quilisma.'

There was silence for a moment.

'Quilisma: what quilisma?' Brother Pragmatius asked with genuine wonder in his voice.

'You know,' the professor said, 'the one in *manes* at the end of the first line.' And here he intoned the phrase *porta manes* in creditable style.

'But there isn't a quilisma there,' Brother Pragmatius answered. 'There isn't one in the entire piece. Heaven knows, the anthem is difficult enough without that, and I might add that most choirs go for the simpler setting of the anthem because the one we sang tonight is just so demanding. As well as awkward intervals, it goes very high, as I am sure you, Professor, who have studied the manuscript carefully, are fully aware. But I can assure you, Professor, there is no quilisma.'

I felt that the tone of the conversation had lost a little of its cordiality.

'Brother,' said the professor, clearly a little irked, 'I can assure *you* that there is a quilisma, and I can tell you how I am so certain. When I was here forty years ago, I spent a long time, some of it with a magnifying glass, making an accurate copy of the manuscript. Because I thought that part of the setting particularly tricky, I checked and double-checked that the composer had wanted a quilisma, and I transcribed the notes as they revealed themselves under my magnifying glass. I am not mistaken.'

There was a slightly frosty silence after this little speech. He then resumed:

'May I ask which text you were using for your rehearsals?'

Brother Pragmatius said firmly, 'What other text would we be using, Professor, if not our own, the original?'

'Do you mean in copy?'

'Yes, of course in copy: you've got the original!'

'But who made the copy?'

'I did. To prepare for this occasion, I made a careful copy of the text and notes from the Hermann manuscript in the two weeks before we sent it up to the auction house. There are only 165 notes in the piece altogether, and I had plenty of time. Don't worry, I know what I'm doing!'

This little altercation ended there, I'm glad to say, but it had already spoilt the end of the evening. The sequel was not long in appearing. The abbot phoned me at the station, a day or two later, in what I should term panic if that did not ill-suit Father Donatus.

'Inspector, I've had Professor Dodsworth on the phone. He is making an astounding accusation. He says that the manuscript he bought from us at auction ten days ago is a forgery: a clever one, but a forgery none the less!'

This was quite frankly astounding news, and you can imagine the jolt to (what passes for) my thought processes. There ran through my mind also, however, quite irrelevant thoughts about the nature of art. If a work of art – say, purely for the sake of argument, a four-page, eleventh-century, German, illuminated manuscript carrying the text of a Marian anthem – is a felicitous combination of form and material which captures a theme in an aesthetically pleasing way, what does its provenance matter? If the Hermann manuscript had been created by, I don't know, an anonymous monk or a socially insignificant goatherd or an archduke in the luxury of his Rhineland castle, how would that have affected the quality of the artefact? Would a later viewer, ignorant of the manuscript's supposed origin, have had any the less satisfying an aesthetic experience? Similarly, if it had arisen in the twentieth century as the work of a talented copyist, would it have been any the less beautiful? tactilely satisfying? odoriferously redolent of busy monks in their scriptoria? Not a whit! The creator, of course, in this latter case, would not be so clever as the original artist, because he would have lacked the inspiration – he might be inspired to create other works of art, but not this one – but how does that alter the nature of the result? I realise that this is a perennial discussion, and I shall spare you any further mental wanderings of mine!

Seven

I eventually got the whole story from the abbot. It appears that the professor returned home that night in a state of high confusion. He rummaged round until he found the copy of the Hermann manuscript he had made forty years previously in the abbey scriptorium. He then compared this with the supposed original that he had bought at auction. There was a discrepancy: the auction copy lacked the quilisma. His conclusion was that he had been palmed off with a forgery – an excellent one in terms of parchment, art-work, pen-work and so forth, but a forgery none the less. He was prepared to stake his reputation on it. As the whole business seemed tied in with the death of Audrey Fletcher, and since the abbot was feeling increasingly out of his depth, would I be kind enough, the abbot continued, to see the professor on his behalf, explaining, not of course that the abbey had put the manuscript up for sale only in response to a blackmail phone-call, but that in a crime of this magnitude, as it was alleged, the abbey felt that the police should be involved to protect the interests of both parties.

I took Blundell along with me to see the professor. He lived in a Tudor house on the outskirts of Lincoln: a tranquil, spacious property surrounded by its own land and therefore set back from the road – which in any case was a quiet one. His books and articles and other academic activities had clearly been lucrative. The door was opened to us by his wife, a horse-faced woman in a tweed skirt and a double string of pearls. The professor had put off the smart suit worn for the previous occasion of our meeting and, now at home, he was casually dressed in corduroy trousers and a thin, brightly-coloured jumper. He was very welcoming. When his wife said she would leave us to our business, he conducted us into his study, brought in an extra chair from the sitting-room and fished the famous manuscript out of his safe.

'Gentlemen, here we have the Hermann manuscript as I bought it at the auction three weeks ago. I understand from the abbot that you were given the chance to inspect it at the monastery.'

'Yes, Professor, we called at Our Lady of the Snows on another matter, and the abbot was kind enough to show us this treasure. We now understand from Father Donatus that you consider it a fake.'

'Yes, I'm afraid I do, and I'm probably the only living person, apart from the faker himself of course, who could make such a pronouncement. You see, I am one of the few people to have examined the original closely in its place of – well, concealment would not be too strong a word, and I doubt whether there is another copy in existence. Here is the copy I made of it when I was a university student forty-something years ago. You can see the date I scribbled on the verso of the last page: 15 February 1911.'

He lifted a few sheets off his desk and handed them to me. Of course, they lacked all the illumination and the feel of the original parchment; and to be quite honest with you, all I saw was an alternate series of squiggles and words.

'How can anybody read this?' I asked. For the first time, I was confronted with the text and 'music' alone, without the distraction of the superb illustrations.

'Well, Inspector, it was just about Hermann's time that the notation of plainsong changed, for precisely the reason you have singled out. As you appreciate, the music, as written out here, is rudimentary, and without later editions in what came to be called *notatio quadrata,* or square notation, it is doubtful whether we would know how the composer intended it to be sung. An Italian Benedictine monk, Guido or Guy of Arezzo, who was an almost exact contemporary of Hermann, realised that the notation in use up till then was really only a loose guide to someone who was already familiar with the melody. So he set about elaborating a system of notation which would be of use to a singer who came to the text for the first time. I'm not boring you, am I?'

'Not at all, Professor! It's quite fascinating.' I took it on myself to speak for both of us.

'What Guido came up with – and I'm simplifying, because he had predecessors in the business, and there were developments in the system after his death – was a staff of four ledger-lines and three spaces, representing intervals of a tone, and notes denoted by little squares or little diamonds. This was very much better than the curves and lines of previous notation, which were quite inexact. He included the pitch and the length of the notes, but he never mastered the matters of rhythm or volume: he left that to the performer. It therefore requires a certain, shall we say, familiarity with the older style of notation to make much of the Hermann manuscript, which to the outsider looks more or less unintelligible.'

'So what is it about this manuscript which leads you to think it's a fake.'

'I don't *think* it's a fake, Inspector: I *know* it is.'

'The abbot mentioned a missing quilisma,' I added helpfully.

'Yes, that's exactly it. In modern notation – and by that I mean *notatio quadrata* – a quilisma is written like a small crown: a black square with a jagged top. In Hermann's time it was most often like a distorted double-u, or sometimes treble-u, with an extended final loop. Quite distinctive, really. Now I know for a fact that there is a quilisma on the seventeenth syllable of *Alma Redemptoris Mater*, that is, on the first syllable in *manes*. If you're familiar with the more ornate version of the anthem, the one that's less often sung because it's a bit of a challenge, it's easy to write out a *clivis* followed by *scandicus* and think you have obeyed the composer's wishes. Or perhaps in this case the forger was distracted, or again genuinely didn't know that the distorted w indicated a quilisma. Now if you look carefully at the Hermann manuscript – the real one, I mean, which unfortunately we haven't got with us - you will see that five tones are crowded together on the one syllable – *ma-* – and that it takes quite careful study to tease the melody apart. Later copies in *notatio quadrata* have interpreted it correctly, incorporating a quilisma, but of course most choirs seem to sing the easier version of the anthem nowadays and don't need to avoid the quilisma, because it isn't there.'

'And you trust your copy of 1911?' I tried to conceal any note of incredulity in my voice.

'I do, Inspector, implicitly. I was a young man, but I was as keen as mustard and very painstaking. I was excited by my visit to the monastery, but I gave myself ample time to do what I had come to do. I didn't hurry, I took no short-cuts, I used a magnifying glass, and I am absolutely, but absolutely, confident that I got everything right. In any case, it would be very much easier to *omit* a quilisma than to insert one by accident. No, Inspector, there can be no doubt whatever that the manuscript you and I are looking at now is not the one I examined all those years ago.'

'And how does it compare with the original in other respects, Professor?' Blundell asked. A very sensible question, which I should probably have got round to asking myself.

'Oh, perfect, I should say. I mean, it feels right, it looks right, it smells right, and so on. The box I should say is the original, but woodwork is not really my province, so I wouldn't care to commit myself on that. The manuscript is definitely a fake, although a very good one, and probably – and I speak without boast – if it had been bought by anyone else, the forgery would have passed unnoticed.'

'May I ask why you don't seem to have established the manuscript's inauthenticity until a fortnight after you bought it?'

'That's a fair question, Inspector, and the answer is that it never occurred to me, not in my wildest imagination, that it was a forgery. I therefore did not inspect it closely. It was only when I heard the monks' rendition on Sunday evening that I suspected that anything might be wrong.'

'And what are you going to do about it, Professor?' I proceeded to ask.

'Ah, well, now you're asking. I should probably approach the monastery and demand my money back – except that they have given it away! I don't think it would be appropriate simply to do nothing, though. What do you advise, Inspector?'

'I agree with you that you shouldn't let the matter go unattended. There's no reason why you should pay good money and in return get a fake. Would you be kind enough to leave the matter with me? I may be able to help. I'll keep you informed.'

My thought was, although I may have been over-ambitious, that if we could find the manuscript, the original, we should have found our murderer.

After the meeting with Professor Dodsworth, I summoned Blundell to a council of war. That is to say, we stopped on our way back to Warwick to discuss the case at a roadside hostelry: so much more civilised, I feel, than my station office or the station canteen. We found ourselves a quiet corner where we could not be easily overheard, in a snuggery of which we were the only occupants but in which burnt a cheerful fire, ordered a modest bite to eat and then sat over our drinks. (I had a cider and the sergeant a pint of bitter: you see, being sure you'd wish to know, I have forestalled your question.) I took my paper napkin, spread it out on the table and prepared to write.

'Let's just jot down the facts as we have them,' I said to get us going, and I wrote:

- a girl whose brother is one of the monks disappears at the monastery – a Saturday in early June;
- her body is found in a shallow grave in the monastery cemetery on the following Wednesday;
- a blackmail message is received on the Friday;
- the Hermann manuscript is taken to London a month later (mid-July) and eight weeks later (mid-September) is sold at auction;
- in early October, its purchaser reports the forgery.

'Now there are obviously a great many things we don't know,' I commented, admiring my handiwork and the clarity with which I had summed up the sequence of events, 'and in the first place they concern the provenance of the forged manuscript: was the copy made before or after it left the monastery, and who knew about it? Ignoring the huge gaps in our knowledge, however, have you had any thoughts, Sergeant?'

'Yes, Inspector, I have. I was afraid you'd be asking me, so I have come up with an idea – but it's so full of holes, I hesitate to bring it out into the cold light of day. You'll think me a complete idiot.'

'Not at all, Sergeant. I am as much in the dark as you, and your ideas are certainly no worse than mine. Remember, I'm new to this job, except as an insignificant acolyte. Fire away!'

'Well, it seems to me common sense to connect the murder with the theft of the manuscript. It's just impossible to believe that these two things happen at the monastery by coincidence, and from your tone I believe you accept that as I do. So here's my idea – and I haven't worked it out properly. The first hypothesis is that Audrey Fletcher, knowing nothing about a copy, was out to steal the original. She says goodbye to her brother at the front door, but instead of leaving the monastery, she disappears off to the library or perhaps the scriptorium – wherever she thought or knew it was hidden. She is surprised in her search, killed and buried, while the murderer or murderess pockets the valuable treasure and makes off. The latter leaves a facsimile behind to obviate suspicion of theft. The second hypothesis, which is similar, is that she is planting the forgery which she has prepared. She is surprised in the attempt to swap the forgery for the original and is killed. I freely confess, however, that both hypotheses are as holey as a garden sieve.'

'Good, excellent,' I said, and I meant it. 'There could be any number of variations on that. We could surmise that she is, for some reason, in the library or the scriptorium, and she surprises someone else hunting for the original. That agrees with your first hypothesis, that she knew nothing about the copy beforehand. Or she catches someone red-handed – an evil-eyed, masked villain with a bag labelled "Swag" on his back: no, I'm joking, of course -- and rushes across to prevent a great loss to the abbey, getting murdered for her pains.'

'But in that case, Sir, what was she doing in the scriptorium, and why does the thief bother to bury her?'

'I can answer your last question: to prevent any suspicion. If the abbot had found a corpse in his library, he would have wanted to know what it was doing there, but with the body disposed of, the hue and cry would be postponed for another day.' I paused. 'Or what about this?' I said, as another idea came to my mind. 'Perhaps, when she feigns to leave the monastery, Audrey lets an accomplice in. The two of them make for the library, or possibly scriptorium, find the manuscript but fall out over it. He kills her, carts the body to the cemetery, to get it out of the way, then does a quick bunk, taking the Hermann manuscript with him. That way we don't have to concoct some unconnected individual wandering round the abbey at sext time.'

'But, Sir,' Blundell protested, 'he just wouldn't have time to dig the grave. And why all the pantomime over the auction?'

'Oh, I don't know, Sergeant, I am really completely bewildered, although there is just one thing that might justify our regarding the Miss Fletcher junior as in some way devious. You remember when we interviewed her brother, he said something like, "When the bell went for sext, she still had one or two things to say, and I was nearly late for office". It looks to me as if she deliberately kept him talking, or at least listening, until the last minute, so that he wouldn't have time to usher her out of the monastery and shut the front-door behind her: that would have scuppered her plans.'

'Yes, Sir. We may not have plumbed the depths of this business, but we have at least suggested some feasible ways in which the two events are connected.'

'Yes, you're right, of course. And our reconstructions have suggested several lines of inquiry.'

'They have? Then you'll have to let me into the secret.'

'Well, we both seem to think that it was possible, or even probable, that Audrey knew either of the manuscript or of the copy, or of both. On the most probable reading of the evidence, she wanted one or other of them for herself, or she wished to prevent someone else from having them. Two questions arise: how did she know about the manuscript and/or the copy? and who was this other person, the murderer? We seem to have ruled out the monks, but who on earth else could it be if it's not an accomplice, or, as we have also suggested, a rival, of Audrey's? So we need to find out about the copy of the manuscript, and my inclination is to start with Brother Jude, since I can't see who else Audrey could have got her information from. If *he* knew about it, where did he get his information from? And I suppose that also means another interview with the lovely Elspeth: I think I might be able to bear that. The second line of inquiry would be to look into Audrey's friends and find out whether one of them might have gone into cahoots with her in a plot to rob the monastery. But I still don't see what good forcing the monastery to put the manuscript up for sale was intended to do – to the murderer, I mean. You'd think he'd just scarper with the manuscript and rejoice in his good fortune.'

All this time, I had not forgotten the murderer's undertaking to hand in to the monastery proof of the guilt of one of the monks. The so-called evidence of the murder, when it eventually arrived, proved, I regret to tell you, a damp squib. The knife was an ordinary kitchen knife, and it fitted exactly the profile drawn up by the pathologist after his inspection of the fatal wound. I had no doubt, therefore, since the details of the wound – indeed the murder itself - had never been made public, that this was the murder weapon. Two factors, however, rendered it otiose. Firstly, it had been wiped clean, blade, handle and knop – whether by the murderer or our blackmailer (if they were not one and the same) I had no means, of course, of telling. Secondly, it was so common a sort of knife that tracing its origin would be quite fruitless.   The piece of monastic habit was a square of coarse material, black, clean, non-descript, with a small trace of blood. It could have been cut from any habit at any time, but for the sake of form, I asked the abbot to look at every habit as it came through the monastery laundry. Nothing, of course.   The blood was the same group as Audrey's, 0+, but also of a third of the population of England, Wales, Scotland and Northern Ireland, not to mention the offshore islands and probably a third of continental Europe as well.   And there were no hairs.

On the following morning, before we began to follow up our identified lines of inquiry, I had a conversation with Blundell – the cauldron of my young and lively mind seething with possibilities, you understand - the tenor of which was as follows.

'You know, Sergeant, a remark of yours yesterday triggered another thought in my mind,' I said.

'What was that, Sir?' he inquired politely, probably not expecting to hear much sense. (Why are subordinates so grudging in their estimation of their lawful superiors? I was not promoted to inspector just for being good-looking, witty, charming and personable.)

'You asked, why the pantomime over the auction?   We had already mentioned the possibility of Audrey being in cahoots with someone unknown. So how about this? The villain is our friend, the not-so-mad professor, harmless enough on the surface, but in reality a cesspit of iniquity. You will have noticed that we have only his word for it that his manuscript is a forgery. For all we know, it's the original, and as he himself admitted, he's probably the only person alive today who could pronounce definitively on that point. His aim is to embarrass the abbey, because, well, let's say because he was refused admission as a postulant in his youth: unsuitable material, he was told: too talkative to be a monk, or too free-thinking to accept discipline, or too radical to adhere to traditional dogmas. This strikes at the very heart of his self-esteem. He nurses a grievance and determines one day, when he is in a position to act, to destroy the abbey. Unfortunately he has no legitimate means to enter the building, so he teams up with an old pupil of his, or more likely the daughter of an old pupil of his, when it comes to his ears that she has a brother in the abbey. He gains entry as we suggested earlier, by exploiting a legitimate visit of Audrey's. He kills her, partly to destroy evidence of his involvement and partly to throw blame on the monks, and buries her deliberately where she will be found quickly and thus puts the abbey into a very awkward position. He then phones the abbot with a blackmail demand, buys the manuscript, which is the original, himself and pronounces it a fake. The abbey is doubly discredited: one of the monks is a murderer, and the abbot passes off as authentic a fake manuscript. It's all pretty ruthless, but it's not beyond the bounds of possibility, is it?'

'Good heavens, Sir,' exclaimed my sergeant. 'We shall be suspecting the abbot himself of murder next!'

'Well, to be honest,' I replied, 'this case is so getting me down, I might end up suspecting myself!'

'What excuse did the professor use to inveigle Audrey into giving him access to the monastery? And why wait all these years before taking his revenge?'

'Sergeant, I don't know. Stop asking so many foolish questions. I may be outrageously fanciful, but I still think we've got to dig a little more deeply into the professor.'

We decided – well, I decided, in a massive show of steely decision-making – that we should split our forces. Blundell and I should see the fragrant Elspeth together, for decorum's sake. Then, while Blundell dug a bit more into the history of the manuscript, I should tackle the professorial end of the tangled skein.

Eight

Because of the suspicions we were harbouring concerning her sister, which could of course be quite unfounded but which we had never the less to propose to Miss Elspeth Fletcher, I felt it better that our 'conversation', as I thought of it, rather than a formal interview, should take place in the privacy of her own flat. We made an appointment, to check that she would be in, and made our way to Warwick. I suppose that she would imagine we came with news of our hunt for her sister's killer, but if so, she was to be disappointed.

'Miss Fletcher,' said I, feeling a little awkward, 'we think our case is making a little progress, but we now need some more information from you, if you wouldn't mind helping us out.'

'Not at all, Inspector. I'll do everything I can, naturally.' She was dressed simply – a blouse and slacks, with a little jewellery – but the effect was undoubtedly impressive. The thought crossed my mind that she was not above wishing to flirt with my young friend Jack. The flat was clean – my perhaps unworthy thought was that it had been cleaned for our benefit, with fresh flowers and a perfumed candle burning – and she made us feel very welcome, offering us tea, which we naturally accepted. (Never refuse a cup of tea: you can never tell when you might have the chance to drink another.)

'My sergeant and I have been reviewing the case of your sister's death, and we have come to certain, not conclusions, exactly, but shall we say possibilities, that we should like to put to you.'

'Yes, Inspector. I'm all ears.'

'We have been puzzling over how your sister was seemingly

attacked inside the monastery – at least, that seems to make most sense - when your brother tells us that, at his last glimpse of her, she was making for the exit.'

'Yes, Inspector.'

'It has occurred to us that perhaps Audrey deliberately stayed inside the monastery, for purposes which might or might not be noble.'

I paused, but there was no further comment from our fair listener.

'Now possibly she met her killer in the monastery, or possibly she let him in herself.'

'Oh, Inspector, what can you mean?'

'Say, for the sake of argument – and I stress that we are still feeling our way – your sister either wanted to prevent an attempt on the Hermann manuscript or, and of course I hesitate to suggest this, had designs on it herself, and she was surprised in the act. You see, the thing is this. Audrey would be quite familiar, after all this time, with the monastic routine. It looks, from remarks your brother made, that she kept him talking until the last minute so that he wouldn't have time to show her properly to the door and shut it to behind her. She would be perfectly well aware that from eleven o'clock she would have a clear twenty minutes while the entire monastic body was safely in chapel. She, and let's say an accomplice introduced from outside, knew, *ex hypothesi*, where the manuscript was. Professor Dodsworth, who bought the Hermann manuscript, thinks his is only a copy. Let us speculate further, then, that, to deflect suspicion, Audrey and her accomplice planned to plant a copy of the original manuscript, in the knowledge that the exchange was extremely unlikely ever to be noticed.'

Elspeth definitely looked a deeper shade of white (if you get my meaning), but for the moment she said nothing.

'So we're tentatively looking for a person who might have acted as Audrey's accomplice. This person, on our reconstruction, then turned on her, taking possession of the real manuscript for himself – or herself, I suppose – and disposed of her body so that, when the monks began to circulate again after the office, nothing untoward would strike the eye.'

When Elspeth still said nothing, I ventured to ask for her reactions.

'Inspector, all this has come as such a surprise to me, I hardly know what to say. You're suggesting that Audrey was stealing from the abbey?'

'Possibly, or possibly stopping someone else from stealing.'

'Oh, I can believe the latter, but to suggest she was a thief is outrageous.'

Ignoring that last bit as the predictable reaction of an emotional person under the impact of a sudden shock, I moved on.

'The problem with supposing that Audrey was acting in the abbey's best interests by preventing a theft is that it is difficult to understand how she could know that somebody else, at that precise moment, was planning to carry the manuscript off. So can you think of anybody who might have persuaded Audrey to cooperate with him, or her, in such a venture as we are surmising? You appreciate that any such person is likely to have wanted Audrey's help to get inside the abbey without being seen and at a time of day when nobody would be about. I'm not accusing Audrey of being the prime mover.'

'Even so, Inspector, it's difficult to take all this in. It's so sudden. Let me think for a minute.'

She mused, taking a sip of tea and nibbling on a biscuit (a custard cream: my favourite).

'Well,' she said at length, spinning the word out to three times its usual length, 'there is one person I wouldn't trust very far, but I've absolutely no proof, and it seems unjust to name someone who might be perfectly innocent.'

'Let us worry about that, Miss Fletcher. This is a murder inquiry, and avenues have to be explored, many of which, mercifully, turn out to be dead-ends. At this stage, we're not making any accusation.'

'Well, I'm thinking of Audrey's boyfriend, Angelo, a creepy, greasy type I shouldn't buy a penguin chocolate from, let alone a second-hand car.'

'Tell us about him, if you would.'

'Audrey met him at some club or other, about six months before she' – slight sob – 'died. He was a good bit older than her, perhaps six or seven years, and worked in a bacon factory on the outskirts of Leamington. Not the sharpest knife in the drawer, but with a certain innate, how shall I put it, deviousness or cunning. At least, that's how he struck me. Quite personable in a way, and certainly handsome, from an immigrant Italian family – Sardinian, I think. But how on earth would he know anything about the monastery, let alone the Hermann manuscript?'

'That's what we need to find out, Miss Fletcher. Do you know where we can find him?'

Our visit to Angelo Costardu that evening was interesting but inconclusive. He lived with his parents in a terraced house that had seen better days: not shabby, exactly, but certainly not smart; not a *cosseted* house. The parents were stereotypically Italian: short in stature, swarthy, running to fat (I did say this was a *stereotype* – I mean no offence to Italians, for whom I have the highest regard), with a broad but not unattractive accent. Angelo himself was undoubtedly a handsome youth, in his late twenties (at least), with perfect English slightly accented – and a numbingly hard hand-shake. After we had settled in the front room, by the looks of it little used and on the chilly side – and I had expressed regrets for Audrey's death, I explained the purpose of our visit.

'Mr Costardu, you knew the abbey of Our Lady of the Snows, of course?' Why give him the chance to deny all knowledge before we'd even begun?

'Yes,' he said, with more than a hint of caution in his voice.

'May I ask in what connection?'

'Because her brother was a monk there, of course.'

'During your time with Audrey, did she ever visit the monastery?'

'Not that I know of.'

'Did Audrey ever talk to you about a particular mediaeval manuscript in the scriptorium there?'

'No, I don't think so.'

'Did she ever describe the inside of the monastery to you?'

'No, why would she do that?'

'Have you ever been to the monastery?'

'No, I'm not even sure where it is.'

'Mr Costardu, have you any idea who might have wished Audrey harm? You must have got to know her circle of friends and acquaintances pretty well.'

'Audrey was a sweet girl, Inspector' – the phrase sounded oddly on his lips – 'and I cannot imagine anyone wishing her harm.'

Back in the car outside, I turned to Blundell with a suggestion.

'Our friend,' I said, 'knows more than he's letting on.'

'How do you figure that out, Sir?'

'I deliberately used the word scriptorium rather than, say, the library. How many people know the word, honestly? Yet he didn't jib at it at all. That suggests to me that it was familiar to him. Perhaps I'm being just too fanciful, as usual.'

'Does no harm to be fanciful, Sir – with respect to your superior wisdom, Sir. I got the impression he was on the defensive: difficult to analyse, exactly.'

'Yes, so did I, Sergeant. Maybe not such an *angelo* as his good looks would suggest.'

Blundell told me two days later what he had come up with in his interview with the abbot about a possible copy of the Hermann manuscript. Here are his own words, as near as I can remember them.

'The abbot was as courteous as usual,' he told me. 'He assured me, in answer to my inquiry, that life in the monastery continued unruffled by the upheavals of the previous month. I asked him about the professor's allegation that his manuscript was only a copy. The abbot did not dismiss the suggestion out of hand. "Possible", he said, "*yes*, quite possible." I asked him to explain. "We have a tradition," he said proudly, "of continuing the mediaeval skill of copying manuscripts. Of course, since the early days of printing, we no longer need to make copies for daily use, but it's a skill we shouldn't like to see die. So monks regularly use the scriptorium for exercising their calligraphic skills." I told him I understood perfectly. He explained that the scriptorium was fully equipped for the work. Nevertheless, I persisted, making a copy of the Hermann manuscript must have necessitated a skill of rare quality. It did, he replied. How many of his monks were capable of it, I asked. "Only one in recent years, to my knowledge: Brother Denis. He's an absolute wizard with the quill on parchment. Methodical, meticulous, gifted. A wonderful illuminator. We have used many of his copies as gifts to friends of the abbey." I see, I said. And remembering Brother Denis' present condition, I asked how long it was since he had made manuscript copies. "Oh, a long time," the abbot conceded. "His eye-sight's not been good for years, and he also found, in his mid- to late seventies, I understand, that his hand was no longer steady enough for such detailed work. So we're talking about at least twenty years ago, I should have thought." Would he remember anything about it now, I asked. "'Fraid not," the abbot replied. "He no longer knows much about anything. A sad state of affairs, but it happens to many." Did the abbot know definitely that Brother Denis had made a copy of the Hermann manuscript? No, he couldn't say he did. If Brother Denis had made a copy, might he have told someone about it? No idea. Could he have made one secretly, without telling anyone? Yes, that is perfectly possible. If he had made a copy and wished to keep its existence secret, where might he have concealed it? Almost anywhere: the scriptorium was full of cupboards and drawers, and no one would bother rifling through all the envelopes and files they contained; or even in his cell, the abbot supposed.

'Remembering your remarks, Inspector, I then asked whether I could have a word with Brother Jude. The abbot excused himself, and I waited on my own in the Blue Parlour for the arrival of Brother Jude. I have to admit that he again struck me as shifty – difficult to reconcile with his sister's powerful aura of honesty.' Hm, I said to myself: quite smitten! 'He was rubbing his hands as if nervously – as if the abbot had mentioned that I should be asking questions about a copy of the Hermann manuscript and he had something to hide. But how far should I let myself be guided by impressions and sentiments? Probably not very far. Except that surely, with experience, one's judgements gained in accuracy, and the clever detective became adroit at sifting out overhasty judgements. Sorry, Sir, I digress: I'm picking up your mannerisms.' I let that one go, as I was anxious to hear what he had to say. 'I put the question to Brother Jude, straight. Did he know whether Brother Denis had ever made a copy of the Hermann manuscript? He looked me in the eye, more or less, and denied all knowledge of any such copy. I asked him whether he'd ever been tempted to try his hand at copying himself. Yes, certainly, and Brother Denis had given him many valuable tips when he had first joined the monastery – before, that is, Brother Denis' mind began to slip.'

I asked Blundell what his final conclusions from his visit to the abbey were.

'Well, Sir, the abbot I think is genuine in his ignorance: he just doesn't know one way or the other. I'm not quite so sure about Brother Jude. It's not much of a conclusion, but I should say that either he knows nothing, or that he knows and is shielding his knowledge from us. Not much help, I admit, Sir,' he added apologetically.

'No, Sergeant. Your conclusion is that he either knows or does not know. I think even Aristotle would go along with that.'

While Blundell was swanning around Our Lady of the Snows, I, of course, was engaged in the serious business of driving to Lincoln to interview the suspect professor: not an interview to which I looked forward with any relish. I had made an appointment, just to be assured that my journey would not be wasted, and he greeted me affably, clearly oblivious of being suspected of a devious and dastardly plot to discredit a group of perfectly respectable monks. Failing that, I hoped to winkle some information out of him concerning the goal of the theft. We sat in his study, and he forestalled me by asking to what he owed the honour of a second visit from me.

'Well, Professor, I wish to be perfectly frank with you. We have no new evidence, but we have been looking at the case from a number of different angles, and I feel I need to fill you in on other aspects of it of which you are probably unaware. I know I can rely entirely on your discretion.'

I let that hang in the air for a moment before giving him a rough account of the murder of Audrey Fletcher, the blackmail demand and the delivery of the murder weapon. I also admitted that no easy answer had obtruded itself into our consciousness. (Did I use that exact phrase? Perhaps I did. Gracious!) Before making my insane accusations – if I was going to - I asked the professor how many people, in his estimation, knew of the existence and value of the Hermann manuscript.

'Well, now, Inspector, that's not an easy question, you know. I should certainly say very few before the auction: a handful of *cognoscenti* who peruse catalogues of libraries' holdings, a few scholars who have studied the history of Reichenau monastery or the life and times of Hermann himself. Say twenty or thirty people in all. From all accounts, the manuscript has been kept more or less secret for most of its life, despite its exquisite beauty and the good chance that it is the work of a holy monk well-known to students of the period for overcoming handicaps that would have submerged many a lesser person. Even those who knew of its existence would probably be unsure of its precise whereabouts today. Of course, the public auction of last month has changed all that. Chapman and Thomas's catalogue did the manuscript proud, but a side-effect of that, obviously desirable from their point of view, is that the manuscript is now very well known amongst scholars who matter. You know yourself the interest that its sale aroused.'

'Yes, Professor, but you will appreciate that for the moment I am interested in the manuscript only before the sale. I don't see how any exchange was effected between leaving the monastery and appearing on the auctioneer's table. That leads me to ask you about your own interest in the manuscript. I remember clearly what you told us at the reception. Could you now tell me how you came to know that the manuscript was at Our Lady of the Snows?'

'Yes, Inspector, that is not a secret.' I thought I detected pity for my ignorance. 'It is listed in various catalogues, since all religious houses were asked years ago to compile some sort of account of treasures they held. I admit that these catalogues, which were originally drawn up for purposes of good husbanding of resources or for insurance, are not easy to come by, but certain university faculties keep them for trustworthy students' – of which I am a notable example, I imagined his adding.

'Had you heard of Our Lady of the Snows before then?'

'No, Inspector, not at all. As I discovered, it is a very small house, tucked away in quiet Warwickshire countryside, and it belongs to an order that has been near extinction for centuries.'

'Had you ever heard of Audrey Fletcher before this evening,

Professor? She was a possible suspect for the role of purloiner of the original manuscript.'

'No, I hadn't. How did she know of the manuscript's existence? And what did she do with it, if she stole it?'

'To take your second question first, Professor, we think that an accomplice took it off her before murdering her. Where it is now is a complete mystery to us. If we knew the answer, we'd presumably have the murderer as well as your manuscript. And the answer to your first question is that her brother is a monk at the monastery. Going on from there, can you think of anyone who would fit the role of accomplice?'

'Can you be a bit more specific?'

'Well, not really. We think the scheme may have originated with this person, man or woman. He or she dreams up a plot to deprive the monastery of its most precious possession, but the snag is that entry into the monastery is virtually impossible without being admitted by one of the monks. This person therefore latches on to Audrey, who has legitimate reasons for entering the monastery, and persuades her to assist him or her in gaining entry. Because the manuscript cannot be sold on the open market, except by the rightful owners of course, I am presuming that the thief had a specific private buyer in mind. The plot goes wrong, in the sense that, if we are right, the accomplice kills Audrey, which certainly cannot have been on Audrey's original agenda, but that doesn't concern us at the moment. What I want to know from you is, can you think of any collector who would resort to underhand means to come into possession of the Hermann manuscript? He or she may not know about the murder of Audrey Fletcher, but he would certainly know that the manuscript would have to be stolen, and by someone both fairly astute and aware of where the manuscript might be held. Any ideas?'

'Well, Inspector, if you gave me a little time, I could perhaps come up with one or two collectors. But please understand that I have absolutely no insight into their morals and so cannot steer you in the direction of any one of them in particular.'

'No, no, I quite understand that.'

I was then guilty of a slight subterfuge, in that I wanted to fish for any more certain sign that Professor Dodsworth knew Audrey

Fletcher beforehand but had not the courage to ask him again outright. I therefore asked him how he had come to be interested in mediaeval plainsong manuscripts, intending to steer the conversation into more promising channels later.

'Ah, well, that's a bit of a story,' he said. 'It goes back to a music teacher at my secondary school. She was explaining how plainsong began to give way, in the fourteenth century or thereabouts, to polyphony. Composers reacted against the simplicity of plainsong, where all the performers sing exactly the same thing, by demonstrating their skill at harmonising two, three, four and more voices in increasingly complex textures. Things got to such a pass that the words became not just obscured but actually lost in the sophisticated staggering of the lines and the interweaving of the voices. That's where Palestrina came in, returning polyphony to a previous simplicity. Mrs Harvey used to play us bits of Machaut, Tallis, Byrd and others, and her view was that polyphonic music was a cut above plainsong: a legitimate and welcome evolution. I began to yearn, however, even as she warbled on, for the simplicity and elegance and beautiful lines of plainsong. So I decided there and then, during a lesson of musical appreciation on Sibelius, it was, that I would study plainsong.'

'So you applied to a university music department?'

'I did. We had to do general music, of course, but we were allowed, indeed obliged, to choose specialisms.'

'And when you came to teach in your turn, did you have pupils who shared your enthusiasm for plainsong?'

'Yes, a few. Most students took my specialist course because they had to take something, but one or two chose to develop their interest.'

'Did any of them become famous?'

'One doesn't become famous in this field, Inspector, unless you count being well-known among a very restricted group of *aficionados* as fame. So, yes, one or two did go on to do great things.'

'Might I have heard of any of them?' This was me getting rather desperate and hoping not to sound like Simon Peter angling for the temple-tax.

'You might have, Inspector, if you have a particular interest in the field. Susan Barlow, Doreen Quickthorn, James Cavendish: do they mean anything to you?'

'No, I'm afraid not.' To lull any suspicions I might have aroused by my clumsy questions, I asked him finally when he retired.

'Twelve years ago, Inspector, after a full and satisfying career.'

'Did retirement come as a shock to you?'

'No, I could at last get on with some untrammelled work of my own.'

Our conversation eventually drew to a close, the professor promising to send me on a list of private collectors of mediaeval plainsong manuscripts, and I was not sure whether I had gained much. I thanked my host and made my way back to Warwick.

I am not proud of this interview with the professor. Had I asked the right questions? Had I missed a valuable opportunity? Could I have extracted more useful information? These unsettling questions nagged at me on my journey home. I beg you, Kindly Reader, not to rush to condemnation. Ask yourself, if you would, whether you would have approached the interview any differently and whether you would have been more successful than I was.

The professor's list of collectors who might be interested in acquiring the Hermann manuscript – and he stressed that it excluded libraries, museums and other specialist bodies – consisted of just three names:

Prof. Rosselli Gianpiero, Il Castello, San Miniato, Tuscany
Dr Nibeaudaud René, avenue des Champs, Grenoble
Prof. Sattler Gerfried, Schultestraβe 47, Geneva.

Since the professor – Dodsworth, that is – would not, perhaps understandably, commit himself to the moral laxity of these collectors, preferring to advocate their moral probity, I seemed to be faced with the task of interviewing all three. On the other hand, it was difficult to envisage that any of them would willingly admit to hiring an agent. I was not even sure yet whether the agent was

Audrey or her accomplice. 'Professor Rosselli, did you by any chance hire a Miss Fletcher to steal a valuable manuscript for you? You did? Excellent! In that case the British police would like a word with you. And could you perhaps tell me, off the record, whether you ever received it? Just for my own satisfaction, you understand.'

I could not decide on my next course of action. What would you have done, I wonder? It is a pity, perhaps, that, because you were absent at the time, I could not profit from your advice. Only you can tell whether you could have steered me in the right direction. In the event, however, my indecision was cut short by yet another dramatic, indeed sensational, development, which I do not think any detective, however astute, could have foreseen.

Nine

It came about in this way. I was sitting disconsolately at my desk the following morning, pondering the lack of progress. There were still two trails I had yet to follow: whether Professor Dodsworth knew Audrey Fletcher or her accomplice, if there was one; and whether his three internationally known manuscript-collectors led us to some maniacal scholar locked away in an ivory tower and keen to commit a felony in the pursuit of his hobby. The first trail might establish the professor's own complicity in the scheme to discredit the monastery. The second was admittedly a long shot. Of the people most likely to create a hue and cry – Elspeth, the professor, the Chief Inspector (although there I was premature) and the press – none was, to my knowledge, demanding a swift resolution to the case, and I was beginning to think that I should return to the Blue Marble Murder and come back to the Missing Quilisma when my head had cleared a bit – in about three years' time. At that moment my phone rang. It was Charles Haydon, an old colleague from our police college days who had risen to the ranks of the CID in Birmingham.

'Hello, Stan, old boy,' he began. 'How are things?'

We chatted a bit about our lives in general: the terrible state of the world, the unstoppable progress of criminal activity, the philosophers' inability to fathom the mystery of the universe, that sort of thing.

'Tell me, Stan,' he said eventually, 'did you ever find that missing girl you were hunting for a few months back, the one with a brother in a monastery?'

'Yes, we did, thanks. Unfortunately she had been stabbed to death and buried in a shallow grave in the monastery cemetery.'

'Are you sure?'

'Of course I'm sure, Charles. Her body was identified by her sister and by her brother. There can be no doubt. There was a funeral service in the parish church followed by a cremation. Why on earth do you ask?'

'Well, there was a traffic accident yesterday in the Edgbaston district of the city. A hit-and-run driver killed a girl, or perhaps I should say a young woman, and disappeared. It happened late in the evening, and I suppose it's probable that at that time of night the driver had had too much to drink. We're actively looking for him, or perhaps her, and we're pretty sure to pick him up eventually. But the thing is, the victim looks remarkably like the photo of the missing girl you posted up in our station in June.'

'Can't do,' I said with some emphasis.

The upshot of our conversation was that I agreed to go over to Birmingham with Elspeth Fletcher and Audrey's former boyfriend, the egregious Angelo Costardu, for formal identification – or not, as I fondly supposed.

The two of them were not both available until the following afternoon. Blundell drove, I occupied the front passenger seat, and our two guests rode in the back. I was not sure whether they liked each other very much, but I considered that irrelevant. We entered the morgue and, after a pause to collect ourselves, we were shown, in a drawer pulled out for the purpose, a body shrouded in a sheet with a cardboard tag on its toe. When we were quite ready, the morgue assistant drew the sheet back from the face. The latter was bruised and flecked with blood, but I admit that it bore an astonishing resemblance to Audrey Fletcher as I had known her through her sister's photographs. I looked at Elspeth and Angelo, both of whom stood there speechless. Eventually, unable to bear the strain any longer, I prompted: 'Well?'

Elspeth hesitated, but Angelo almost blurted out, 'Yes, that's her! I'd know her anywhere!'

I asked them whether there was any distinguishing mark by

which identification could be made more certain: a scar, a birth-mark, a physiological peculiarity. Angelo said, without hesitation, 'Yes, she had a crescent moon tattooed on her lower back'. Elspeth nodded in agreement. With the assistant's help, we turned the body over, and there could be no doubt about the presence of a tattooed crescent moon surrounded by a halo of stars. That seemed to me to be decisive. I had originally intended to fetch Brother Jude in, reluctant as I was to disturb the monastic routine yet again, but I now saw no need to do so. Let the monk continue at his prayers.

The body was returned to its former composure and shut away. We walked quietly back into the lobby.

'Miss Fletcher,' I said, 'I'm very sorry that your sister should die in this way. But I must ask you why you were so certain that the body we found in the monastery cemetery was Audrey. Neither you nor your brother seemed to be in any doubt.'

'I don't know, Inspector. I was very upset, the face was battered, the clothes and the ring on her finger were quite definitely Audrey's, and it just never occurred to me that I was mistaken. She had gone missing in the monastery, she was found in the monastery. It all seemed to make some ghastly sort of sense.'

The assistant handed me a handbag containing the deceased's effects. There was a library ticket in the name of Jayne Templeton; a driving-license in the same name; a letter from the bank addressed to Miss Jayne Templeton, of 3 Westbourne Road, Edgbaston; and so on. I looked at Elspeth, but only strain and bafflement showed on her handsome face. She was, one would have said, stupefied. Angelo was perhaps less shocked, but he too was clearly shaken by this latest turn of events. Neither of them had any explanation as to why Audrey should surface dead – again – and this time under an assumed name. I realised that a long inquiry lay ahead of me.

On my return, I found that the Detective Chief Inspector had issued a summons for my presence. DCI Clive Maxwell was a man in his forties, of robust build, with an intelligent face, ears too big for him, and a square chin that jutted out in intimidating fashion. His office was a lot plusher than mine – naturally. He motioned me into a chair and began, without preamble, by asking me how I was getting on with the Murder in the Monastery affair, as he called it.

'Not very well, Sir, as it happens.' I was still reeling from the afternoon's discovery.

'Tell me about it,' he said, not unkindly.

I related all that we had done and found out in the preceding months, of some of which he was already aware: the search of the monastery and grounds, the discovery of the body, its identification by the girl's siblings, the menacing phone-call a few days later, the decision taken by the monks in chapter, the auction of the Hermann manuscript, the service of celebration in the abbey chapel, the professor's contention that his purchase was a fraud, the bombshell of this afternoon. I kept nothing back, dreading that I should be demoted as being out of my depth but hoping that I would be reprieved and even given a little assistance. I told him that we had come up with a number of possibilities that we were actively – save the mark – exploring, and that the afternoon's astonishing revelation could provide just the clue we needed to bring the case to a close. I obviously sounded confident and enthusiastic enough to allay the DCI's suspicions that I was completely at sea and a dead loss to the force, because he merely enjoined me to persevere, to leave no stone unturned, to keep my nose to the grind stone, and other like phrases. He said he had high hopes that I would see my way through the labyrinth. In the meantime, I was to take on no other work but to concentrate on this one case. He wanted a result before the professor began jumping up and down for his money and accusing the force of incompetence.

'Yes, Sir, of course, Sir.' I felt like a teenage pupil dragged up before his head teacher for persistent weak performance in the classroom. 'I am going to suggest to your parents, Wickfield, that you go down a class and repeat a year. Perhaps you'll improve with maturity.'

I left the DCI's office in no very cheerful mood, as you can imagine. Instead of clarifying matters, the latest revelation seemed only to make them more obscure than ever. Fortunately, I was saved a great deal of trouble by another summons to appear before the DCI on the following morning.

'Look here, Wickfield,' he said, 'we've had an inquiry in from the Coventry police, who in turn have received an inquiry from the Polish police in Łódź. It concerns a girl from the region whose family are worried about her because they haven't heard from her for six months. Perhaps you'd care to read the report that has just come through. I understand that the first part has been reliably translated from the Polish by a native speaker whom the Coventry police have used before.' He leant over his desk with a sheet of paper in his hand. This is what I read:

The family of Jadwiga Zawadzki, of Orszewice (the hamlet is too small to have separate addresses for the houses – our apologies) have asked us to contact you because they have concerns about their sister who went to Coventry four years ago to find work. At first she kept in regular touch, even managing to send a little money from time to time. Latterly, however, they have heard nothing, and it is not at all in her character. Her last letter, of six months ago, told them that she was still working in a factory making electric kettles and that she had taken up with a fellow-Pole called Henryk, surname unknown. It also hinted that they might be moving because Henryk had been promised a better job.

She is 24 years old, of average height and build, long black hair, a round face, brown eyes. Was considered pretty in her village. She spoke no English when she left Orszewice but had a little German. She intended to find work in Coventry because she had heard of a distant relative working there. The latest address we have for her is Flat 4, 27 Eagle Street.

We [the British police] made inquiries of the Polish church in Coventry, and the parish priest, Fr Gorzyński, was very helpful. He remembered the couple very well and spoke highly of them. He confirmed that they had left the parish some eight to nine months previously, and he thought that they had gone to Warwick but couldn't be sure. He hoped no harm had come to them. He was able to give us Henryk's surname – Krawiec. We hope that this information, scant though it is, enables you to pursue the search for the girl. Her family are clearly anxious about her. We are happy for you to pass on to us any information gleaned to be forwarded to the Polish police.

'Well,' the DCI commented when he had given me time to peruse this sheet, 'you seem to have two bodies where you thought you had only one, and I wondered whether this information might be of interest to you.'

There being here at least a definite course of action which promised a positive result, I ascertained without more ado the present whereabouts of young Mr Henryk Krawiec – I presumed he was young – and found his flat, only to be told by his landlady that it was foolish of me to expect to find him at home during the day, because he worked. She did, however, have the grace to tell me where he worked: MES (Mellington Exhaust Systems) at Bridge End, off the Banbury Road. Taking irrational exception to the woman's caustic comment but hot on the trail, I drove post haste to MES and contacted the manager. In cases of this kind, I saw no reason not to intrude on the works' routine. Henryk appeared, dressed in grey overalls. I took to him at once: a loose-limbed, clean-living sort of guy, I said to myself, the sort one would like for a son. (My elder son was then five years of age, so a direct comparison would have been fanciful.) A shock of brown tousled hair surmounted an open face; clear eyes; generous mouth; regular white teeth. On the other hand, our conversation, being unproductive, reminded me in some way of my interview with Professor Dodsworth: would I ever acquire the knack of interviewing people, suspects or not, *fruitfully?*

We sat in a room that seemed to function simultaneously as a waiting-room, a corridor and an adjunct to reception. He was ill at ease, but that is readily attributable to my imposing presence.

'Mr Krawiec,' I said with what I hope passed for quiet amiability, 'we are trying to trace a Polish girl we understand you knew in Coventry: Jadwiga Zawadzki – sorry if I'm not pronouncing that correctly. Her family have contacted the police to say they are worried, as they haven't heard from her for over six months. Can you help us?'

'No, I'm afraid I can't, Sir,' Henryk replied, a little stiffly. His pronunciation was good. 'You see, Jadwiga and I parted company shortly after we came to Warwick.'

'Would you like to tell me more?' I said, not willing to leave our conversation there.

'We moved to Warwick with my job. We found a flat – the one I'm living in now. After about a week, Jadwiga had not found work. She suddenly announced to me that she was going back to Coventry, and she left.'

'Just like that?'

'Yes, Sir. I was very disappointed, but it was her life. We were not, as you English say, an item. And I've not seen her since.'

'Have you heard from her in the last six months?'

'No, Sir, nothing.'

'Any idea where in Coventry she went to?'

'No, Sir, sorry, I have no idea.'

I could not winkle any more out of him, and I felt profoundly disillusioned. From the sketchy description of the girl given in the Polish police report, she might easily have passed for Audrey Fletcher, particularly if the face were subject to a few judicious punches to disguise dissimilarities.

My next port of call was the address of the late Audrey Fletcher, also known as Jayne Templeton. Having obtained the necessary search-warrant, Blundell and I drove the few miles to Birmingham and found our way to the deceased's flat in Westbourne Road, Edgbaston. I had two things in mind. We were going to look first and foremost for the original Hermann parchment, accepting, for the purposes of the exercise, that there was a copy in existence and that that's what the professor had. We were also looking for any indications of the identity of an accomplice. If we were not totally wide off the mark, Audrey had been responsible, in part or in whole, for a theft, a blackmail, a murder and a surreptitious and daring burial: not a bad tally for a middle-class girl in her early twenties. She would almost certainly have needed assistance in some or all of these exploits, and I was determined to find out.

The flat was small, comprising three rooms: a kitchen, a bedroom, and a living-room. If Audrey had made a lot of money by selling the manuscript on, there was no hint of it here. We set about our work systematically, working through boxes, cupboards and cabinets, under the bed, the undersurface of tables, behind pictures: we were very thorough. We found nothing incriminating, no hint of dark deeds, no evidence of criminal malpractice. Surprisingly, we found nothing either of her former identity, except that the dressing-table was smothered in cosmetics and the wardrobe full of smart clothes, which we guessed had been the hallmark of Audrey Fletcher, certainly if her sister was anything to go by. We returned to the station with, I've no doubt, disappointment only too apparent on our young and innocent faces.

The discovery of the identity of the victim of hit-and-run accident had, however, opened up other avenues of speculation which we had not yet explored. (I am aware that purists dismiss 'exploration' as a heuristic strategy, but we shall not quibble with them here.) I therefore decided to review the case with Blundell in the light of the recent developments.

'OK,' I said, 'let us two do some serious thinking. We have quite a few facts before us, and it should not be beyond our combined wits to conjure up some sort of explanation with an indication of where we go next. Let's go back to the monastery – in our minds, I mean – to that day in June when Audrey was supposed to have disappeared. What think you?'

'Well, Sir, we have to look at two hypotheses.' Good, I thought. Here's a man who is logical and organised. 'On the first one, there was no theft. Audrey left the monastery in the normal way and, for reasons of her own, disappeared. Perhaps she was fed up with Elspeth's controlling her life and longed to be on her own, to start life afresh. We then have the problem of the burial of the body in the cemetery. On this hypothesis, Audrey had nothing to do with it. On the second hypothesis, however, there is a theft and Audrey is responsible. She makes off with the manuscript, and a body is somehow planted in the grounds to divert suspicion. The blackmailer must have been aware both of the murder-cum-burial of the unfortunate Jadwiga and of the Hermann manuscript, at least the original. On this hypothesis, it stands to reason – well, almost – that

Audrey was in the whole business up to her neck. Her disappearance surely points to that.'

'Good, very good,' says I, 'but I think we have to exclude the first hypothesis, if you don't mind my saying so.'

'Why is that, Sir?' – very polite but visibly irked.

'Because it strains our credulity to breaking point to imagine a complex plot involving – possibly – the theft of the Hermann manuscript and its substitution and the burial of a female body on abbey grounds without Audrey's involvement. Both theft and murder-burial point ineluctably to the hand of outsiders: we have uncovered no evidence whatever that any of the monks had either opportunity or motive for either crime. It is beyond belief that Audrey does a vanishing act on the spot, so to speak, and yet is completely innocent.'

We sat in silence for a while, until an idea gradually dawned in my mind. Light did not exactly come flooding in, but it trickled in as the germ of a thought.

'Hang on a minute, Sergeant. We've been supposing all this while that Audrey Fletcher was done to death in the abbey and her body smuggled out to the back while the monks were at sext: a gap of less than twenty minutes to accomplish quite a lot. Also, the murderer would have had to make good his escape – or her escape, of course; I keep forgetting - without being spotted. Now that we know for certain that Audrey survived to live another day, what is there to stop us from thinking that the body in the cemetery was planted there, say, the previous night? We know that Jadwiga was stabbed to death. If this was in the scuffle in Chapel Street, Warwick, witnessed by our Bible-reading old lady on the Thursday, why can't we say that the body was taken off the street and carried to the abbey any time in the next forty-eight hours – or more probably thirty-six – and buried under cover of darkness? I bet Audrey's appointment with her brother was not made until the Friday for the following day. You see, if she had nefarious designs, she couldn't or wouldn't put them into effect until the scene was properly laid, and that included her supposed body growing cold in the abbey cemetery. So she couldn't apply to meet her brother until after the burial, and then she had to allow another twenty-four hours for her appointment. At some stage they, whoever "they" are, had to dress the body in Audrey's clothes and knock the face about a bit to disguise it.

Saturday was really the first day after Jadwiga's death that a meeting with Brother Jude, which gained her legitimate entry into the monastery, could be engineered. Now we're getting somewhere, Sergeant!' I concluded triumphantly.

'Aren't you being a bit hasty, Sir?' said Blundell. This was very deflating, but I took the blow on the chin.

'Why is that, Sergeant?' I asked with, in the circumstances, admirable restraint.

'You haven't explained anything about Jadwiga's death, which remains as much of a mystery as ever. How did her body move from lying in the street to the abbey grounds? Did some motorist, who happened to drive up Chapel Street at that precise moment, say to himself – or herself, of course – "Hey ho, there's a body. Let's drive it out to Our Lady of the Snows and give it decent burial. And while we're at it, let's just keep the murder weapon in case we find a use for it later". On the other hand, if you think murder was committed to order, so to speak – "We need a body quick, let's murder that girl over there" – how were they to know she could be passed off as Audrey? No, Sir, in my opinion there are just too many holes in your theory.'

'Look, Sergeant,' I said rather acidly, 'I'm floundering, the same as you are, but at least I can suggest where we might go next.'

'Yes, Sir, where's that, Sir?'

'Nobody came forward locally to report Jadwiga missing. Does that not strike you as strange? No boyfriend, no place of work. I put it to you that young Henryk has told us a pack of lies. Despite his denials, he was the boy with Jadwiga when she was attacked. The other woman was the new love of his life, and Jadwiga was murdered to make way for her. Henryk is holding out on us because he suspects that we are going to pin the murder on him, or use him to trace his girl-friend who wielded the knife. Neither of them can be positive that the old lady saw much of the scuffle, could identify the participants or went to the police, so they don't know how much – or little – we know. Unless – ' I paused pregnantly as yet another idea rose effulgently from my mental cornucopia – 'unless the new love of his life was Audrey! Henryk or Audrey or both were struck by the similarity between Audrey and Jadwiga and concocted a plan to put pressure on the abbey to sell the manuscript. That's it!' I said excitedly, as I warmed to this new reconstruction. 'If Henryk and

Audrey simply stole the manuscript, the loss might be noticed, but if they forced the abbey to sell a copy and then kept the original for themselves, the loss to the abbey would not be noticed. It was just their bad luck that the manuscript was bought by the one person in the world who recognised it for what it was, a forgery. However, they could not persuade the abbey to sell their most precious treasure by normal means, so they hit on an ingenious plan involving murder dressed up to look like an inside job, thus putting the abbey into a compromising situation. The added bonus was that it got rid of Jadwiga, who was proving too much of a limpet and obstructing Henryk and Audrey's new life together. Great stuff! I think that just about wraps it up!' I beamed in triumph. Blundell looked less than impressed.

'Yes, Sir,' he said with a distinct lack of enthusiasm.

'Dammit, Sergeant, you just don't wish to acknowledge brilliance when you hear it. You're jealous, I do declare, just because my brain works more subtley than yours.'

'No, Sir. I mean, yes, Sir. But you have to admit that you have not a shred of evidence in your favour: not one teensty, tiny, weeny piece of evidence. I'm not sure you'd convince a judge and jury.'

'Very well, Sergeant, have it your own way. You know better than I do, I daresay. I'm just a muttonhead.'

'The emotions are not always immediately subject to reason,' commented William James, 'but they are always immediately subject to action.' I beg to differ from the great psychologist. My emotions act on me, and I seem powerless to control them. Does civilisation encourage us to stifle emotion or to exploit its energy? Should I be seeking to destroy feelings or to channel them? Pass.

In the end I shook off my petulance, and we drew up a plan of campaign, in no particular order of priority. All the tasks had to be performed before we could risk the fiasco of further unprovable reconstructions(!).

- the first thing to do was to interview Henryk at the station, formally. He must know more than he was letting on.
- secondly, we had to know more about the accident in which Audrey was killed. It was supposition on my part - but then I

was a Popperian and believed in supposition – but I wondered whether it was an accident or deliberate murder designed to remove an encumbrance.

- thirdly, we had to follow up the professor's list of collectors. We could not afford to neglect any aspect of the case which promised information.

- fourthly, we needed to reconstruct the burial of the body in the abbey cemetery: was it feasible to park on the main road, carry the body through the woods and bury it in the abbey grounds, all in the dark and without being heard or seen?

- fifthly, we needed to establish with certainty whether the professor could have known Audrey, or perhaps Audrey's mother, which might indicate that he was part of the conspiracy to defraud the abbey.

- sixthly, and finally, we needed to get another expert opinion on the status of the Hermann manuscript in the professor's possession: if it was possible to adjudicate in the matter, could it be the original or was it definitely a later copy?

Ten

Henryk Krawiec was invited to present himself at Warwick Police Station for formal questioning in connection with the death of Jadwiga Zawadzki. I was determined to conduct the perfect interview: no undue hectoring, no shouting, no threats, no lies, just rational discourse, man to man. If he was innocent, bullying was unjust. If he was guilty, cool reason was more likely to persuade him to come clean than intimidation. Perhaps I am naïve.

'Mr Krawiec,' I began, after the usual caution and when I had seen Blundell start the tape-recorder, 'I am sure you are as keen as we are to establish the truth concerning Jadwiga's death in Warwick on 2 June. I want you to go over carefully again what you told us a few days ago about your move with Jadwiga to Warwick.' I had made sure that a jug of water and a plate of biscuits stood available to Henryk: psychology, you understand.

'Inspector, I know no more than what I told you before. I was given promotion provided that I moved to the firm's new premises in Warwick. After discussion with Jadwiga, I agreed with my boss to do so. We found a flat, we moved in, I started my job. A week later Jadwiga said she was bored at home, she was going back to Coventry where she had spent the previous three years, and that was that. I didn't argue. She went. That's all I know.'

'You told us before that she left no forwarding address. I find that hard to believe, Mr Krawiec. How long had you been together?'

'I had known her for a year.'

'But inhabiting the same flat in Warwick was not the first time you had done that, was it?'

He hesitated. 'No, it wasn't,' he admitted.

'So when did she first move in with you?'

'About six months after we met.'

'Whose idea was it?'

'Can't remember. Both of us had the same idea, probably.'

'But you told us you weren't, in your own words, "an item". What is living together if not being "an item"?'

'All right, we had an understanding.'

'An understanding that you might get engaged?'

'Yes.'

'Then I just don't accept that she walked out on you. Weren't you dumbfounded?'

'"Dumbfounded"? What is that?'

'Weren't you astonished that she could walk out on you, after just a week in the new place?'

'Yes.'

'Didn't you make any attempt to persuade her to stay?'

'Yes.'

'But you told us before that you let her go without an argument.'

'Yes.'

'Look, Henryk, you'll have to do better than this. We're not getting anywhere. I don't believe she left you at all. Did she?'

Henryk looked utterly forlorn.

'No,' he whispered. 'She would never have left me. We loved each other.'

I waited for him to take control of himself.

'So what happened?'

For a while he could not bring himself to speak. Then he told us.

'Jadwiga and I had gone out for the evening: just a drink in a pub, you know. We couldn't really afford any more than that. We were on our way home when we were approached by a woman with a knife. We didn't know she had a knife at first. By the time we found out it was too late. She attacked Jadwiga, who fell to the pavement.

The woman fled in one direction, I in another.'

'Right, I can believe you so far, Henryk, but there are two things I don't understand. The first is, did you know this woman? Of course you did. What was her name?'

'No, I didn't. I swear it. She knew Jadwiga and said that Jadwiga had taken the job she'd wanted. "Bloody foreigners taking our jobs," she said, or something like that.'

'You told us Jadwiga hadn't been able to get a job.'

'I know. It wasn't true. She got a job serving in a newsagent's.'

'Which one?'

'"Skellon's, in Jury Street.'

'Right, we can chase that one up later. My second question is this. Why didn't you report the murder?'

There was silence.

'Didn't you think it important enough?'

Still silence.

'Come on, Henryk, I need to know. Why didn't you report Jadwiga's murder? If you didn't even know the woman's name, you can't have been shielding her.'

'Inspector.'

'Yes, go on, I'm listening.' I was getting just a little bit impatient. Henryk was hard going.

'Inspector, I didn't want any trouble with the police: I haven't got any papers.'

'You mean you're working illegally?'

He hung his head.

'Yes,' he said in a whisper.

I realised then that that probably explains why the newspaper shop had said nothing to us either: they were knowingly employing a foreigner without papers and were afraid it would come out in any investigation. It transpired, after further questioning of Henryk, that both he and Jadwiga had, independently of course, got one year visas and that they had stayed on after the visas' expiry, frightened of repatriation if they applied for an extension.

I continued the interview.

'Did you know what happened to Jadwiga's body? Do you know now?'

'No, I have no idea. I presume that somebody would have called the police and that they would have seen to the burial.'

'Didn't you think to write to Jadwiga's family? You had her Polish address, I suppose.'

'I did. Of course I did. We'd planned to go back to Poland for a visit, to celebrate our engagement.'

Two tears trickled down his cheeks, and I felt desperately sorry for him.

'So why didn't you write?'

'Because they would have told the British police, and then I would have been found to be without papers.'

I then told him about the discovery of Jadwiga's body at the monastery, its mistaken identity and the cremation of Jadwiga's remains. I told him I did not think there would a problem with re-labelling and re-locating the ashes if he wished it.

Despite his misery, I had to pose the question of his possible acquaintance with Audrey. 'Henryk,' I said, 'I want a completely honest answer to my next question. A lot may depend on it. Do you know – did you know – a woman called Audrey Fletcher, very similar to Jadwiga in build and looks, lived in Warwick, aged 24?'

'No, definitely not. I've never heard the name before.'

'Are you quite sure?'

'Yes, quite sure. All our friends in Coventry were young Poles who went to the same church as we did, and in Warwick we got to know only other people at work. Jadwiga never mentioned anyone by that name, and I certainly didn't work with anyone called Audrey.'

'What about Jayne Templeton: did you know her?'

Henryk shook his head. 'No, I've never heard the name.'

'Angelo Costardu?'

He shook his head again.

I believed him. Wouldn't you, even without the benefit of visual contact? So ended our – my – interview with Henryk Krawiec. I felt satisfied that I had achieved my purposes. The murderess of Jadwiga could now, no doubt, be identified and dealt with by the courts, and our investigation into the Murder at the Monastery was slightly, ever so slightly, advanced. Krawiec's illegal status was not, at that moment, high on my agenda.

I determined next to beard the not-so-mad professor in his den. It was a rainy day in November when I steered the car up the drive of the professor's Lincolnshire residence. Everywhere was damp and disconsolate. Dead leaves lay in soggy heaps. The trees dripped. The house looked melancholy, staring out on to a wet, late autumnal world. In contrast, the professor's study was warm and cheerful, with a fire in the grate and the air of a much lived-in space. Heavy curtains alongside the windows, a thick carpet, heaps of books, a desk littered with papers, several deep armchairs, a small table containing a decanter and several glasses all spoke of a comfortable retreat from the world's anguish. Since I was about to challenge the owner's claim that his expensively-won piece of parchment was a copy, and possibly accuse him of a deep-laid plot to close down a monastery, I needed to tread carefully.

His wife offered me a cup of tea 'to wet my whistle' after a long journey on a dank morning and promptly disappeared, leaving the professor and me to our awkward *tête-à-tête:* awkward for me, that is, probably not for the professor.

'Inspector,' he said genially, 'this is an unexpected pleasure! I don't receive many visitors these days, not out here, and particularly not such distinguished ones.' A young detective inspector from Warwick CID, distinguished? Come off it, Professor! However, I would match bonhomie with bonhomie.

'Professor, I can assure you that it is an equally great pleasure for me to be here again. I've come to pick your brains.'

'Oh, yes, I'll certainly help if I can, you may be assured of that. I take it you're having a bit of trouble.'

'Well, we're making progress, but there are some loose ends we're anxious to tie up. For a start, I think that a close examination of your Hermann manuscript might reveal more about the forger. That's probably an inappropriate word, because there is as yet no case for accusing him of express intent to deceive. As you probably know, the monastery made copies of illuminated manuscripts in their possession to dispense as gifts to particular recipients. If you wouldn't mind, I'd like to take it away with me today and subject it to tests by experts to see whether we can't pin down characteristics of the copyist.'

'Well,' said the professor benignly, 'I see no reason why you shouldn't, but it's still worth something, even though it's not original, so be careful with it.'

'Thank you, Professor, I appreciate that.' I was not done with my duplicitous questions yet, but I was so nervous, I was afraid of betraying my real intentions. 'Now you told me,' I continued with what I hoped was unstudied nonchalance, 'how your interest in plainchant was fired by a music teacher at school. Did you never contemplate the monastic life? After all, in an order like the Benedictines – or the Gilbertines - five hours a day are spent singing plainchant.'

'Just let me correct you there, Inspector. The Benedictines are not "an order" in the usual sense of that word: Benedictine monasteries form a loose federation, not a unified organisation. But why do you ask, Inspector?'

Oh, Lord, he hasn't rumbled me already, has he?

'I would value your opinion on a matter that's been puzzling me. What I need is the opinion of someone like yourself, acquainted with the monastic way of life but not committed to a particular loyalty. I'm trying to estimate the likelihood of a monk's, or a whole abbey's, deliberately passing off a copy as an original rare manuscript, but if you've never been part of a monastic community, I'm asking for an excessive stretch of the imagination. You see the point of my question?'

Had I assuaged the professor's suspicions sufficiently to encourage him to betray his grudge against Our Lady of the Snows?

'It's astute of you to guess, Inspector, but I confess to you that between school and university I did spend a year with the Cistercians at Westvleteren Abbey in Belgium – just to try it, you know. I was young, enthusiastic, idealistic I think one might say, but it wasn't for me. I couldn't have coped with the celibacy, for one thing.'

'May I ask why you chose Belgium and not somewhere nearer to home: Mount St Bernard's, for example?'

'There was no particular reason, Inspector. I fancied a location which was, shall we say, slightly exotic to a boy reared in East Anglia: sheer pretension, now I look back on it.'

'The Gilbertines, an East Anglian order, never appealed to you?'

'As I told you, Inspector, although I knew of them historically, because I was brought up for some of my childhood not very far from Sempringham, I had no idea there was still a Gilbertine foundation in existence. If I had known, perhaps my life would have taken a different course – despite the difficulty with celibacy. I discovered the existence of Our Lady of the Snows only during my university studies.'

'And can you conceive of a whole monastic chapter conspiring to palm off a copy as an original?'

He thought for a moment. 'A lax monastery might in theory, but then you'd be more likely to get factions breaking out and treacherous moves of one faction against another. That might be conceivable in pre-Reformation times, but not since, I should have thought.'

'Thank you for that, Professor. May we now turn to Audrey Fletcher, whom I mentioned to you before as a chief suspect in the case?' I decided to say nothing about her death – her second death, that is - which was irrelevant to our present conversation.

　　And we see that the departed

　　Have no place among the living.

(*The Song of Hiawatha*, Faithful Reader, if you did not spot it.)

'Did Miss Fletcher approach you at all as a possible purchaser of the Hermann manuscript?'

'Why should she?'

'Well, Professor, I'm embarrassed to confess that before this case came my way, I had never heard of you. You are, as I have discovered, famous in your own sphere, but my interests had never lain in this direction before. For Audrey, however, a purchaser for the manuscript was essential if her plan was to succeed. Of course, all this is absolutely between ourselves: I have no proof of her involvement in any crime, I am merely seeking the truth. Now, on one possible understanding of the facts, Audrey Fletcher conspired to steal the abbey's most expensive manuscript and to sell it for a substantial sum. She could best do this by approaching a known collector and offering it at below market value. She would benefit from a quiet sale, the purchaser would benefit from a discount. In fact, the manuscript is unlikely ever to have been sold at all without her intervention – still working on a hypothetical reconstruction of the plot, you understand. Now if Audrey was looking for a buyer, she would naturally make it her business to seek out likely collectors. She need never let on that theft was at the bottom of the scheme. She could always have come out with some story about the abbey wanting to sell, but discreetly, through the agency of a trustworthy partner of the abbey like the sister of one of the monks. That way, the monks would have no contact with the outside world and could exploit the knowledge of someone less unworldly than themselves; and the buyer could buy in completely good faith. So, did Miss Fletcher approach you at all, Professor?'

'Inspector, no one approached me with an offer before the sale of the manuscript by Chapman and Thomas. I went into the auction prepared to bid against other interested parties without the slightest advantage. Open market conditions prevailed, certainly as far as I was concerned. I have seen and heard nothing since that has changed my view of the matter.'

The professor gave me the impression of telling the truth, although of course, if he were involved more deeply than he was letting on, he would naturally do his best to convey his unsullied innocence. Was this a case of the serpent pitted against the dove?

I came away from the professor's house dubious, but for a reason I could not fix in my mind. However, the immediate task facing me was to submit the manuscript of which I was now in possession to rigorous testing. I made my way to the Gibson-King Laboratory in Cambridge and asked to speak with a Dr Serafin, with whom I had made a previous arrangement. Now Dr Katriana Serafin did resemble a mad professor. Her ginger hair, which struck one first, reached for the ceiling in wild clumps. Her rimless spectacles were perched on the end of her snub nose as she peered over them to speak. Her clothes were assembled, seemingly, from items randomly selected at jumble sales. Her long fingers were never still but clutched each other in permanent frenzy. However, there was nothing mad about her approach to scientific analysis, which was, if I am any judge, workmanlike and professional.

'Ah, Inspector,' she greeted me enthusiastically, 'welcome! I believe you have something interesting for me?'

I believed I had, but I enjoined on her the utmost discretion, since the case was still in progress (I made bold to use that word again: she was not to know differently!).

'Yes, Doctor, I believe I have.' I flourished the wooden case, placed it theatrically on the bench and opened it with choreographic precision.

'A nice piece,' she said. Taking the manuscript in her gloved hands, she leafed through the pages, admiring the workmanship and savouring the overall sense of masterpiece that pervaded it. 'Right,' she added, 'what do you want from us?'

'I will not conceal from you, Doctor, that there is dispute in a murder case over whether this manuscript is what it is claimed to be.'

'And what is it claimed to be?'

'It is said to come from the abbey of Reichenau on Lake Constance, or Bodensee, as our German friends have it, and to have been drawn up somewhere between about 1030 and 1050. The author is said to be a monk who goes by the name of Hermann the Cripple, or Hermannus Contractus.'

'Have you other examples of his work, authenticated, with which I can make a comparison?'

'No, I'm afraid not. You see, if we are right, this manuscript is unique, in that Hermann wrote poetry, but we have no evidence he had illuminating skills. As a monk, he would probably, almost undoubtedly, have been initiated into the rudiments of illumination, but no original work of his has come down to us - that we know of. The tradition of its provenance claims Hermann as the author, not just of the words, for which it is historically known he was responsible, but also of the music, at which he was proficient, so that is more than possible, and also of the execution of the whole manuscript. A lot of money depends on its authenticity, Doctor.'

'So?'

'So I want you and your colleagues to subject the manuscript to whatever tests you need to to ascertain its likely date and place of origin. You will pay particular attention to the age of the parchment, the style of the art-work, the style of the penmanship – if it was a pen that was used, and not a reed or a quill – the age of the paints, the availability of the dyes at the supposed time of its composition. Come on, Doctor, you know all this better than I do!'

'Yes, yes, Inspector, but I want to be sure we are giving you the information you require. How long have we got?'

'Twenty-four hours?' I answered, facetiously.

'Give us a week,' she said, 'and I'll ring you when we've got something for you. These things take time, you know, and we've plenty of other things on hand at the moment.'

'Just one other thing. You might also look out for fingerprints. If it's a copy, I am fairly certain I know who might have handled it, but I should like to be certain. There are probably more than one set of prints in any case.'

I shall tell you now, Patient Reader, the results of the tests performed for us by the Gibson-King Laboratory. This is, for the second time in this narrative, to override my intention to tell the story in strict chronological order. You are favoured, because I value your continued attention: I should not do this for everybody. The report came back with a lot of sophisticated jargon about chromatography, spectroscopy, enzyme reactors, archaeometrics, graphology, electron microscopes, the ultrastructure of parchment and goodness knows what else besides – all way over my head, I need not tell you – but the end result was inconclusive. The excellent condition of the manuscript was attributable to its being housed in a tightly closed wooden box and rarely handled. The parchment was genuinely eleventh-century, and the pigments and calligraphic styles were consistent with German traditions of the time. There was a lot of other information on the nature of the parchment (calf-skin), the origin of the dyes (possibly Meckenbeuren), and so forth. If it was a copy, it was a very clever one, the work of a master in the field, and they would like to meet him! The boffins had also isolated several sets of finger-prints, photographs of which they included with the report.

Eleven

While I was thus engaged, Detective Sergeant Blundell was organising a re-enactment of the burial of Jadwiga according to the *modus operandi* we had envisaged. Depending on the time that elapsed between her death and her burial, her body would be more or less stiff with *rigor mortis*, or, alternatively, quite flexible. Certainly in the former case, we felt that two carriers would be required. We also thought that, if one of the carriers was Audrey, the other would be a man, and there were a number of possibilities to fill that role: Brother Jude, Professor Dodsworth, Angelo Costardu and others we had not yet identified. I was not there, of course, but I relay to you the scene as he told me about it afterwards.

The props that Blundell organised comprised a clothed life-size body weighing roughly what Jadwiga weighed, a winding-sheet, a torch and two spades; a map, a stop-watch and a camera. The personnel were a police-woman and a police-man, and Blundell himself with the watch and the camera. A study of the map quickly revealed the most likely route taken by the two plotters on that June night six months before. From the south-bound carriageway of the A46, two tracks led off into the woods that covered the Cass Valley, both ending in gates into abbey fields, and of the two tracks, one was significantly nearer the abbey buildings. A car reversed into the track would very quickly be invisible to passing traffic as it moved back towards the gates. It was thought that the most likely time for the plotters to act would be between two o'clock and five o'clock in the morning, if passing traffic and hours of daylight were the only considerations. Abbey activities, however, offered a more restricted window, and between two and three in the morning was considered more likely. The abbot and monks were taken into their confidence and asked to report any sounds or sights impinging during the operation: not on special watchers, you understand, but on monks sleeping contentedly and guilelessly in their cells. The police had also been allocated an undisturbed plot in the cemetery in which to dig their grave.

At the appointed time, on a still November night with only owls for company, the police-car reversed into the woods, the rear lights shedding enough light for their purposes. It would have made little difference, it was thought, if the original car had driven forward into the woods and reversed afterwards on to the main road. Perhaps the decision would have depended on whether there was any other car on the road at the time which would have noticed a vehicle slowing down or reversing in such a spot in the depths of the night. Working in silence, the two constables opened the boot, removed the body, tied their spades to it and waited for their eyes to adjust to the darkness. They then clambered over the gate, which was locked, took the body by the shoulders and feet and made their way down the field toward the abbey buildings that loomed up a couple of hundred yards away. They moved steadily so as not to trip or stumble with their burden. They skirted the orchard wall, stepped on to the track that led from the garden to the fields and followed it a little way until they came to the gate in the cemetery wall. This they opened very slowly, in case it squeaked – which it did, but almost inaudibly. They laid their body down, unstrapped the spades and set to work digging a grave just over two feet in depth. The walk down the field had already warmed them up, loaded as they were, but digging even a shallow grave in double-quick time brought the perspiration to their foreheads, although the night was cold. When they had dug deeply enough – two spades' depth – they lowered the 'body' in, heaped the earth on top, stamped it down, and scattered the remaining earth on the grass. They found that they had had to use the torch but little. The spades had made noise whenever they encountered a stone, but it was impossible to tell, from where they stood, whether such noise could be heard as far away as the dorter. All this time Blundell was recording the event with his flash camera.

Having concluded their macabre business, they smoothed the grass and earth round the grave with their spades to erase footprints and in this way backed out of the cemetery on to the track. They left the 'body' in place, so as not to distort the timings, and headed back for the road with their tools, retracing their steps on the track, across the field and over the gate into the wood. Blundell recorded that the entire operation, from door to door, so to speak, had taken twenty-three minutes. Later that morning, the team returned to the abbey, emptied the grave and checked with the abbot whether any of the monks had heard or noticed their activity. None had. Blundell concluded, quite rightly in my opinion, that his reconstruction would persuade a jury that they had uncovered the route and the method used by the plotters to plant Jadwiga's body in abbey grounds.

Then Blundell sprung a surprise on me. I was peeved not to have thought of it myself, but I admired him for his initiative: credit where credit is due. He took the opportunity, while he was at the abbey with the team, to re-enact Audrey's possible movements in her appropriation of the Hermann manuscript. He acquired from the abbot, who had no difficulty in producing one from the abbey's stock, a monastic habit of the right size, and then Blundell directed the demonstration, stop-watch and camera in hand. He reasoned that Audrey neither would nor could wander round the abbey in her own clothes, whether her original entry into the building had been legitimate or not. His first thought was that she would hire a costume from a theatrical outfitter's, but he immediately spotted two flaws in that arrangement. Firstly, it was very unlikely that any outfitters would carry such an unusual habit. Secondly, its acquisition by Audrey could very easily be traced. He therefore concluded that Audrey would have made her own, perhaps in a light-weight material that could be stored easily in a bag. As far as footwear was concerned, open-toed sandals on a warm June day would attract no attention whatever. For the purposes of the exercise, Brother Jude was represented by the police constable, Audrey by the police-woman.

The three of them assembled in the Blue Parlour, and when the bell for sext sounded, 'Brother Jude' and 'Audrey' continued to talk for a few minutes. Then 'Brother Jude' led the way out, ushered his 'sister' towards the front-door, but instead of seeing her out, doubled back and made for the chapel. 'Audrey' then returned silently to the Blue Parlour and proceeded to disguise herself with the habit hidden in her bag: cassock and scapula, a girdle and a set of rosary beads. The bag, now containing only the fake manuscript, was tied round her waist *underneath* her habit. Pulling the cowl up over her head and folding her hands in her sleeves, she moved out of the Blue Parlour and headed purposefully but quietly towards the kitchens. At one point Blundell had to halt the re-enactment, because he feared that her haste, unbecoming in a monk, would draw the attention of any hypothetical real monk who happened to be in the vicinity. The 'monk' set off again at a more composed pace. Instead of entering the kitchens, 'Audrey' made for the scriptorium. There she took from her bag a supposed replica manuscript, exchanged it for the supposed real manuscript in its box, put the supposed real manuscript into her bag, and left the scriptorium. Instead of returning the way she had come, she walked meditatively to the rear door of the abbey, entered the garden, took the track that led out past the cemetery into the field and retraced her path of the previous night. When she was safely in the shelter of the wood, she resumed her own appearance by replacing her props in her bag. The entire exercise had taken nine and a half minutes.

This little scene had the advantage of proving what really we already knew: that Audrey's time was not excessively generous. The implication of that was that she had to have known beforehand where the manuscript was. There simply would have been no time to carry out any sort of meaningful search in the scriptorium or the library, much less both, or even make her way to Brother Denis's room and search there, bare though the cell would be. It was, in that sense, an inside job; and I began to suspect Brother Jude. Now that we knew that Audrey escaped from the abbey with her life, we had no need to argue the existence of an accomplice who turned on her, murdered her and buried her in the abbey cemetery; but she had to know where the manuscript was hidden if she was to leave the abbey grounds before the conclusion of sext. She could hardly risk being caught rummaging in the library or scriptorium during the singing of Divine Office, much less wandering about the dorter searching for Brother Denis's room. There was some risk in the operation clearly, but it had to be minimised. I congratulated Blundell on his reconstruction. A fine piece of work, I told him; but why on earth had I not thought of it myself? Very humbling.

Blundell's next job was to catch up with the motor accident in which Audrey Fletcher lost her life. Audrey, living as Jayne Templeton, lived at 33, Westbourne Road, Edgbaston, off the Harborne Road. Uniform had done a perfectly workmanlike job in assembling the facts as they were known. Most of the information concerning the accident itself was provided by a single eye-witness, but surrounding detail was available from others. By day, Audrey worked for Courtauld's, in their research department. In the evenings and at weekends, she attended dancing classes at the Curzon School of Dance and night classes in painting at an off-shoot of the Birmingham Institute of Art and Design. She also entertained – it was thought, female friends from work – and went to the cinema several times a month. There was not, seemingly, a steady boyfriend. This information was provided by the tenant of the flat below Audrey's, with whom Audrey had friendly but not close relations.

I have often wondered what it is like to live under an assumed name, to adopt, in a sense, a new persona, to pretend to be who or what one is not. Actors, of course, do it all the time, but then, for one thing they are trained, and for another, they do it for short periods of time only. Sherlock Holmes, if we are to believe his creator, was an adept at it – and so was the man with the twisted lip! To adopt a different identity for long periods, to close oneself to one's past for fear of betraying oneself, to establish a new web of friends and acquaintances, is quite another kettle of fish and seems to me to require a determination and a stamina above the ordinary. Audrey must have had pressing reasons: flight from the past? fear of imprisonment? the lure of a glamorous future? How curiously some people's minds work!

On the evening of her death, Audrey had been into town by bus. The neighbour thought she had been going to attend the preview of an art exhibition: wine and nibbles and a guided tour of the works on display: you know the sort of thing. Blundell did not think it worth our while to check which venue it was and whether Miss Templeton had in fact attended, and I agreed with him. Police resources are not so abundant that we could afford to waste them on issues that were clearly not essential. The bus, a No.55, dropped her off on the Harborne Road, twenty yards from the top of her own street, at a little before ten. The place was well lit. As she entered Westbourne Road, a car, identified provisionally as a red Austin-Healey, came out of Westbourne Road in something of a hurry, cut the corner and clipped Audrey on its way. She fell, striking her head on the garden-wall of the first house in the street. A woman on the opposite side of the street happened to be drawing her curtains at that moment, saw the accident and phoned an ambulance. However, by the time the ambulance arrived, the victim was dead. The identity of the car was tentatively established on the basis of the woman's description, but, despite inquiries and interviews, the driver was never brought to book. It is not even certain that he would have known that he hit a woman, as, by the time of her fall, he was already out of sight round the corner. It was a dangerous and inexcusable piece of driving, but difficult to call intentionally homicidal on the evidence available.

I was downcast by the number of times in this inquiry our leads led to ambiguous conclusions. There seemed never to be data on which we could stand and echo Luther. The ground shifted all the time, suggesting now this, now that, possibility. A great deal of lateral thinking (I apologise for the anachronism: I don't think the term had been invented then!) would be needed to unravel our mystery.

There remained one and a half items from our agenda of three evenings before: whether Professor Dodsworth was telling us the truth when he denied knowing either of the Fletcher girls; and whether his list of international collectors gave us a clue to the purpose of the theft. The first half point was answered in a curious way about which I shall tell you in its place. For the moment I focussed on the collectors. They were three, if you remember: an Italian professor from Tuscany, a French doctor from south-east France and a Swiss professor. Fortunately, I was able to eliminate the last of these three very quickly, on the basis of an astute phone-call to the auctioneers Chapman and Thomas. I had wondered who Professor Dodsworth's underbidder was, and the auctioneers told me it was Professor Sattler from Geneva, with whom they were familiar from previous sales of mediaeval manuscripts. I reasoned thus to myself: a man who attended international sales and was prepared to pay international prices either did not need to, or had the integrity not to, resort to criminal means to increase his collection. I may be wrong on the principle, but in the case of the Hermann manuscript, I felt my reasoning was correct.

I therefore got clearance to interview Professor Rosselli and Doctor Nibeaudaud. Quite how I was going to persuade either of them to admit illegal ownership of the Hermann manuscript I was unsure, but it was an avenue we had to go down. I could, I suppose, perhaps even should, have left the task of interviewing these gentlemen to local constabulary, but the DCI was anxious to extend my experience. Another consideration, he told me, was that only I (and Blundell) were in possession of the full background to the case, and no amount of explanation to our Italian and French colleagues, it was thought, could easily convey the nuances and side-roads of the investigation. I therefore found myself, on a grey November day, heading for Pisa airport, where a police car was waiting to drive me out to San Miniato, between Pisa and Florence. The weather was fine, and the half-hour journey scenic and intensely pleasurable. The Arno Valley was bathed in weak sunshine, and the olive groves reflected moving patterns of greys and greens. As we climbed up from the valley floor, I saw the fortifications of the town loom up ahead, and then the Renaissance palaces, the *duomo* and the splendid *palazzo comunale*. The castle is today more of a tower, reconstructed after war damage but still impressive – or perhaps more impressive than ever.

I was received by Professor Rosselli, when I had finally gained admission to the *Torre*, leaving the driver to divert himself as he might in the cafés - or museums or shops - of the town. I hoped my Italian, perhaps supplemented by his English, was sufficient for what lay ahead. The professor told me, as we settled in his sitting-room, that he had retired from teaching fine art at Florence University and felt free to indulge his passion for the mediaeval art of illumination. Family money, he led me to believe, augmented his university pension. He offered to show me his collection, and of course I eagerly

117

accepted.

'I have fifteen tenth- and eleventh-century manuscripts,' he told me with pride, 'and forty from the next three centuries. Not all of them are in good condition, and one or two are hardly legible in places, but I bought them for their art-work rather than their text, so that does not bother me.'

'Do you allow scholars access?' I asked with diffidence becoming (I thought) in one so unaccustomed to this level of scholarship.

'Yes, of course, Inspector. Florence University has a list of my holdings with permission to forward reputable scholars whom they have vetted. I have a small but regular stream of visitors wishing to view this or that manuscript.'

The room in which we were seated, with windows on all four sides and an internal staircase in one corner leading to both upper and lower floors, was magnificent. There was a huge open fireplace, bookshelves, display cases covered with felt to keep out the light, heavy occasional tables bound with ornamental metal: a sumptuous room. I felt both awed by its splendour and privileged to glimpse the ivory tower from within.

'And are your visitors at liberty to browse, or do you fear damage from clumsy hands?'

'Inspector, I make my entire collection, both of manuscripts and of books on art, some of them, ahem, my own, available to serious researchers without restriction. I have a supply of gloves – just in case, you understand, although reputable scholars nearly always arrive properly equipped - and I am always present when these people are working. I do not see the point of owning such wonders and yet not sharing them with my colleagues.'

I gazed with fascination as he displayed, firstly, the codices and manuscripts in the cases, which he said were his choicest works, and secondly, those in the various drawers which he opened for me. The subjects of the illuminations were divided equally, I thought on my quick overview, between sacred and secular, many of the latter mythological in nature.

'Tell me, Professor, do you know of the manuscript containing the *Alma Redemptoris Mater*, said to be the work of Hermann the Cripple, and held at the abbey of Our Lady of the Snows in England?'

'Oh, yes,' he said. 'I've never seen it, and the only facsimile I've seen is the first page in the auction catalogue, but its historical associations are quite fascinating. Why do you ask?'

'Did you know it had gone on sale recently?'

'Yes, I knew,' he said. 'Chapman and Thomas always send me their catalogues when mediaeval manuscripts are for sale.'

'May I ask why you didn't go the auction to bid?'

'How do you know I wasn't there, Inspector?'

Since I could hardly tell him I was there on the abbey's behalf hoping to spot a murderer in the crowd, I just told him I had been present and found it all extremely interesting and had spent a lot of time gazing round at those attending and bidding at the auction. This seemed to satisfy him.

'I guessed it would go for a lot of money, and at the moment I am concentrating on other areas of mediaeval manuscripts. So I stayed away in case I was tempted beyond my means!'

'Tell me, Professor, do you know of anyone who would attempt to steal the manuscript because he couldn't afford to buy it?'

'What a strange question, Inspector, but I suppose that is the main purpose of your visit. The world of mediaeval manuscript collectors is a rarified one, and it is inhabited, I guess, by the scholarly and the aesthetic and the discriminating. I say that without affectation. None of the collectors I know - and I meet many at all different levels of enthusiasm and means at auction rooms – would stoop so low. On the other hand, one can never be 100% certain. A collector who was set on possessing the Hermann manuscript would, in my circle, have written to the abbot to ask whether it was for public sale or whether the abbey would consider an offer. Theft would be a desperate resort. I have to add, however, that I'm not sure whether many people knew of its present whereabouts. You see, it has never, to my knowledge, been featured in illustrations, and although it is listed in international catalogues, it is listed without details. It would need a special kind of expertise to appreciate its real value in the circumstances.'

I was more or less persuaded by the professor's logic, although I should perhaps have phrased it differently. He was arguing, if I comprehended him, that collectors of beautiful things were above the commonplaces of theft. Stated thus baldly, the evidence of history was against him. On the other hand, identifying the rogue collector in the fraternity of mediaeval manuscript enthusiasts was a different question. Any such person would be expected to conceal his proclivities and conquests from his fellows and present to the narrow world of collectors, as to the wider world of outsiders, a façade of irreproachable integrity. In that sense the professor was right to admit only rare cases of lapse. My impression was that he himself was above reproach. If he genuinely allowed scholars to browse in his collection, he had nothing to hide. Of course, there was only his word. How difficult is the assessment of character!

Anyway, I took a cordial leave of Professor Rosselli and embarked on a pleasant train journey to Grenoble via Florence and Milan to visit Dr Nibeaudaud. The latter was a very different person. Whereas Rosselli was urbane and aristocratic, Nibeaudaud was timid and fractious, the product of his own exertions (I told myself). His house was the typical *maison bourgeoise* of French towns, indistinguishable from its neighbours. Madame Nibeaudaud greeted me at the door – a stooped, fragile creature in a long frock, with shaking hands but a thoroughly amiable face – and her husband, short in stature and not the smartest individual on whom I have ever clapped eyes, led me into the salon. His voice was querulous, but his manner impeccable.

We talked about mediaeval manuscripts, their attraction as investments and *objets d'art* for the connoisseur and the fragility of human existence as exemplified in the transience of the illuminator's art, and it was then he who came to the point.

'I understand, Inspector,' he said, 'that your visit concerns a manuscript in particular which you think may have been stolen to order. I gathered as much from you when you made the appointment to see me. Which manuscript do you have in mind?'

His French was precise, almost precious, that of a well-educated man who lacked the advantage of breeding (if it is an advantage). I told him as little as possible of the case but as much as he needed to know to make a proper judgement.

'We have reason to believe, Doctor, that Manuscript GB – OS An 7, commonly known as the Hermann manuscript, was stolen six months ago from an isolated monastery in central England. We think it may have been taken to fulfil the commission of a collector, but whether British or continental we don't know. Could be American or Australian, I suppose, but your name was given to us as that of one of the few scholars in Europe with the necessary knowledge to help us further.'

I waited expectantly.

'Inspector,' he said, weighing his words, 'I'm not sure I can help you very much. You see, the Hermann manuscript is known in its full glory to few. It has been in England, in a monastery, out of sight of scholars, for hundreds of years. It has never been shown in illustrations, as far as I know, and since it was moved from East Anglia at the time of the Reformation, it is even more remote than before. To my knowledge it has been described just once, in a book called *Ars Pictoris Bavariensis in Medioaevo*, published in a limited edition in Munich in 1607. This book is extant in a single copy, and it is of course in Latin: not a very helpful source of information to many today. As I say, there is no accompanying illustration, just a brief verbal description extolling the manuscript's virtues. I know this because I am the owner of this single copy' – and he gestured to a bookshelf locked with a grill. I was suitably impressed.

'So what is your point, Doctor?'

'My point is that so few people know about it, the usual percentage of one rogue per hundred collectors – or whatever percentage your Francis Galton might have calculated - cannot apply! No one would risk a theft for a manuscript they had never seen. My advice to you, Inspector, is to go back to the abbey where this manuscript was kept – Our Lady of the Snows – and ask the abbot how many people have asked to see it in the last few years. That could be the lead you've been looking for. Of course, the Chapman and Thomas catalogue, which they are always kind enough to send me because I have bought at their auctions before, has changed all that. Scholars are much more aware now not just of the manuscript's existence but of its importance – and, what is more to the point, of its worth. So the insurance on it will rocket.'

This made sense to me. We continued talking for a while. He was not so easy an interlocutor as his Italian counterpart in Tuscany, but he was none the less very interesting on his subject – or perhaps I should say on this subject, because I never did find out what his academic speciality was: medicine, for all I know, or law, or philosophy, or theology; or music, perhaps. We parted on good terms – I hope I had made myself agreeable – and I returned to England in a better frame of mind, ready to tackle the next phase of the inquiry.

Twelve

Several things needed our attention: the finger-prints on the Hermann manuscript photographed by the Gibson-King laboratory, the visitors to Our Lady of the Snows who had asked to see the manuscript, and any possible connection between Professor Dodsworth and Audrey Fletcher. None of them, probably, would furnish the break-through we needed – except that one could never be sure. I also told myself, in my more sanguine moments over a pot of tea, that, as in some chemical reactions, it was not the last ingredient added, but the particular *combination* of ingredients, that was important.

I spent the morning after my return from Grenoble catching up on paper-work and writing a report for the DCI (who was getting agitated, I imagined – not about my safety, you understand, jeopardised by so much unaccustomed foreign travel, but about progress in the case), while Blundell was to phone the abbey and check on the finger-prints. At lunch I strolled out, in wan late-November sunshine, to sit in a café over a sandwich and a cup of tea and to think, when, to my astonishment, I saw a man and a woman sitting over lunch in an establishment I had intended to pass by. Nothing unusual in that, you say, and in the normal course of events you would be perfectly correct. These two, however, were both known to me in the course of the present investigation: Elspeth Fletcher and Jack Blundell. Kindly Reader, please do not judge me harshly when I tell you that my first, instinctive, reaction, oblivious (such is the male psyche) as I was of the fact that I was a happily married man with two young sons, was jealousy: how come the taciturn Blundell had hooked the handsome Miss Fletcher? Blundell was acceptable in his way, but surely Wickfield cut the more dashing figure? Casting these unworthy and foolish thoughts from my mind, I moved on to consider that the sergeant's liaison with Elspeth was disturbing the equilibrium of the case. She was not a suspect, but was it wise to be taking up with someone so intimately connected with it? Was it indeed *professional?* As I stood there, debating these questions within myself, Elspeth waved, and I had either to pass on, perhaps with a sign of acknowledgement, or enter the café. One option not open to me was to continue to stand on the pavement with my mouth open and a vacant expression on my face: I could tell from my reflexion in the window that I was beginning to look ridiculous. In no more time than it takes for a detective inspector to come to a brave decision, I had entered the tea-shop and asked the couple whether they minded if I joined them. Blundell stood, with only a few signs of awkwardness, while Elspeth was as suave as ever.

'Inspector, you don't even need to ask,' offered Elspeth. 'You are naturally very welcome. We were just talking about you, as a matter of fact, weren't we, Jack?' Not so much as a wink in Blundell's direction, so perhaps she was telling the truth.

'Oh, yes,' says I, picking up my lead so artlessly thrown out by the fair lady, as I drew my chair from under the table preparatory to making myself comfortable, 'and why was that?'

'Jack was just telling me you had returned from Italy and France, on both occasions speaking the local lingo like a native.'

'The sergeant is very kind,' I replied, a little more stiffly than I had intended, 'but I am not so fluent as he is suggesting. German's more in my line.'

Three thoughts went through my mind. Who had initiated the little scene of which I was now a part? Was it right for Blundell to be discussing the case, in however oblique a manner, with Miss Fletcher? And why did Elspeth exercise such a fascination on the male of the species, me included? Deciding that now was not the time to follow up these questions, I determined to contribute manfully to a merry little threesome.

They had only just ordered, so I made haste to follow suit, and we sat round the little table as if there were no murder, blackmail and forgery between us, just a budding intimacy in a relaxed moment. I looked carefully at Elspeth. Her make-up was artful: so little that one wondered whether she had any on, and yet enough to highlight the lustrous eyes, the charming nose, the firm chin, the expression of come-hither freshness that reached deep inside one's gut. She was wearing a Swiss-style jerkin and a neckerchief, and a long skirt. She and Blundell were not yet, at least not in my presence, what in vulgar parlance is termed 'lovey-dovey', but their attraction seemed to be mutual, and, as I gained control of my emotions, I began to wish them well.

'Tell me, Elspeth,' I said ' – I may call you Elspeth, mayn't I? – I am wagering that Warwick isn't your birth-place. You seem too sophisticated for a small Midland town.'

'My,' she said, 'I can see you've been to police college!' I couldn't take offence at this put-down: I had asked for it. 'But you're right, in a way. I was born in Carlisle; we all were.'

'And when did you move to Warwick?'

'It's a long story, Inspector, you don't want to hear it.'

'Oh, but we do,' interjected Blundell enthusiastically. Oh, dear, he was not going to embarrass me with his ardour, was he?

'Well, Inspector, if you wish to know, I am happy to tell you that my father was headmaster of a school in Carlisle, and we were brought up, naturally, in the headmaster's house in the grounds – or at least it was then incorporated into the grounds. It was a handsome house, purchased by the governors when it was thought that the then head's accommodation did not quite fit the image of the school they wished to project. What had been the head's house, which was part of the main building, was then given over to specific school use.'

'And you attended that school, of course?'

'We did. It was really two schools, boys' and girls', with one head.'

'And did you like it?'

'Yes, very much. I'm not sure that Audrey was quite so keen: her memories didn't seem to be so rosy as mine, but I loved my school days. The boys enjoyed it too, on the whole. I did well academically, I was in several sports teams, and I was a member of the school orchestra. Before you jump to the conclusion that I was any good musically, I should perhaps tell you that the school started up an orchestra in my time. My father's decision, of course, but he was nagged into it by a parent whose son was a talented trumpeter. He advertised the establishment of an orchestra and invited pupils to volunteer. Two violinists and a flautist did – and the trumpeter, of course. That was all. They could, no doubt, have found music for that unlikely combination, but it was not quite what the words "school orchestra" bring to mind. By this time my father was not going to let what he regarded as his scheme collapse for want of response, so he bullied the governors into purchasing a range of instruments so that prospective players wouldn't have to buy their own. As one parent aptly pointed out, nobody would commit himself to the purchase of an instrument if there was a chance he wouldn't find it to his liking. So eventually my father was able to tell the assembled school, We've got an oboe here – flourishing it – or a cello, or a clarinet, whatever it might have been – who would like to try it? The response this time was positive, and in no time at all – well, two years, I suppose – we had the makings of an orchestra. Looking back, I can tell you without shame that we were dreadful! But all schools have to start somewhere, don't they? I daresay it's an excellent ensemble now, ten years on, tackling Bartok and Stravinsky and goodness knows what else. How on earth did I get on to telling you all this?'

'No, no, all very interesting,' I said. 'But if you were all so settled there, why did you move?'

Elspeth's face fell a little.

'Well, Inspector, you see, Jude, Audrey and I had another brother, between Jude and me: Oliver. He was a quiet, studious sort of boy, a bit of a dreamer. He took after our mother and wanted to be a painter, a creator of works of art that would stun the world with their originality and sense of colour and form; I don't think beauty came into it, which is perhaps a pity, but there you are. He never really fitted in with his peers, because he was, well, weedy, and hated sport, and wasn't rough, and he mooned about, thinking and dreaming, inhabiting a world of his own. The terrible thing was that he suffered from depression: black, hopeless bouts of it that used to tear him – and us – apart. There was nothing anybody could do. The psychiatrists prescribed some sort of drug, can't remember now what it was, and it doesn't matter anyway, but it never seemed to do much good. He went away to art college, in Newcastle, and just towards the end of his three years, he was at home during the Easter holidays. He told us that he couldn't cope with the examinations that he was due to sit that May. He didn't turn up for supper one evening, and Dad, who went in search of him, perhaps because of a prescient sense of foreboding, found him hanging in the gym.'

'How awful!' exclaimed Blundell.

'It was,' Elspeth went on. 'It sent the family into a spin, I cannot describe to you. Audrey, who was perhaps closest to him, was particularly badly affected. Dad would have gone to pieces if he hadn't had the school to look after. He never again set foot in the gym, and he handed in his notice to the governors immediately. He got a job at another school here in Warwick, but he died two years ago, just as he retired.'

Blundell and I maintained a discreet and sympathetic silence.

'And your mother?' asked Blundell.

'Mum took it very hard as well. I was nineteen, Audrey only sixteen, and Mum stayed calm for her sake.'

'You said your mother was an artist,' I said to Elspeth. 'She didn't do those paintings in your flat, did she?'

'Oh, no, they were Oliver's. Mother painted in a much more traditional style: woodland scenes in the mist, bowls of cut flowers, thatched cottages under snow, that sort of thing. She was good enough to hold a number of exhibitions, though.'

'Would I know her?' I asked.

'You might,' Elspeth said, 'depending on how interested you are in modern artists. She exhibited under her maiden name, Sheila Morton.'

I shook my head.

'Did any others of you take up painting?' asked Blundell, I suppose artlessly, but I could not be sure.

'Jude was interested. He wasn't bad, but going into a monastery he had to give up that type of thing.' My ears pricked up, as you can imagine. I said nothing but stored the information away.

'If Jude went into a monastery, does that mean you were a religious family, Elspeth, or just Jude?'

'Both Mum and Dad were Catholics. We were all brought up as Catholics, but as happens, it sunk more deeply into some of us than into others. I'm not particularly religious now, nor was Oliver. I believe in God, but I don't really go along with organised religion. Too much of it as a kid, maybe. I'm not anti, just nothing really. Now Audrey was different. She was very religious. Used to get on my nerves a bit, to be honest.'

Here she paused. 'I think I've said too much.'

'No, you haven't, Elspeth. Let me complete your thoughts for you,' I said gallantly, 'to show you that I was a step ahead of you. Then you won't feel so bad.'

She hesitated. 'Do we have to go on talking about this?'

'We're there now. Look, I need to know. Audrey, I think, was killed for what she knew. Perhaps she threatened to go to the police, or perhaps her killer just thought she might go to the police. You can help us find him or her by being honest. All right?'

'Yes, all right,' she said quietly after a bit.

'I think this, then. Oliver's death hit Audrey hard. She had perhaps been praying for a solution to his illness. When he died by his own hand, she turned against God, against religion, and against priests. She couldn't master her grief, so she decided to take it out on the closest group of Catholics she knew: the monks of Our Lady of the Snows. How am I doing?'

'I think that's guess-work, Inspector. She *did* turn against God, but I never heard her threaten anything or anybody as a consequence. She just kept her sorrow to herself. Occasionally she would come out with some phrase critical of religion or of Bible-bashers, but she never did so when she was still at home: that would have hurt Mum and Dad something dreadful. Since then she seems to have recovered her poise a bit.'

'But you would not be *very* surprised if I could prove to you that she was involved in some plot against the abbey?'

There was an inner struggle, manifested in a change of manner and a sigh.

'Inspector, if you could prove that to me, I should accept it reluctantly but with good grace. But the thing is, you can't prove it.'

'No, I can't, but it looks the most likely case at the moment. I'm sorry if I am causing you grief on the basis of unfounded suspicion. There's one final question I'd like to put to you, Elspeth, if I may.' I came out with this after a short pause. 'Have you any reason to suspect that Audrey knew Professor Dodsworth?'

'Professor Dodsworth?' she said. 'Who's he?'

'The collector who bought the Hermann manuscript at the Chapman and Thomas auction.'

'Oh, him! Is that what his name is? With a surname like that, I bet he's got a sumptuous Christian name like Zeredah or Eleazar!'

'Don't be facetious, Elspeth! Could Audrey have known him?'

'Well, if she did, she never mentioned him to me. Why do you ask?'

'Nothing, really. Only trying to clarify my ideas a bit by swamping them with useless information.'

At that, I rose from my chair, collared the waiter for my bill and left Elspeth and Jack to it. I hoped I was building up a clearer picture of the family. From the beginning of my police career, I have taken an interest in the motives for which people turn to crime, and while Freud may be on the wild side, I agree with him that the springs of 'evil' – for want of a better word – reside in one's experiences as a youngster – or perhaps I should say in a combination of personality and experiences. This is not an original thought, but it is probably true none the less. If Audrey was half so charming as her sister, and if the whole family were essentially religious, law-abiding and conventional, only something grave could have disturbed the tenor of her personality. Of course, I was prejudiced against her, because my investigation had suggested, very forcibly, that she was the prime mover in an unpleasant sequence of events, but I was also keen to judge her fairly for her sister's sake. Oliver's suicide had not swept her siblings into a life of crime, so why Audrey? Because her character was already flawed. Unfortunately, Audrey was no longer with us to tell us in what way it was flawed.

After the lunch-break, Blundell came slightly sheepishly into my office and asked, quite properly, I think, whether I wished him to discontinue to see Miss Fletcher. I did not know quite what to say, as I was in two minds, so I simply told him that I had rather he had waited until after the end of the case.

'Is that a yes or a no, Sir?'

'Look, Sergeant, I suppose it's all right, but you couldn't keep it very discreet for the time being, at any rate, could you? Don't make too much of a thing of it, if you know what I mean. And whatever you do, don't discuss the case with her!'

'How will I know when the case is ended, Sir?'

'I hope you're not being flippant, Sergeant. It's ended when we've got an arrest and a conviction – you know that.'

'And what if we don't get either, Sir?' I think he was quite serious, but since I could no longer be bothered to give him a civil reply, I just grunted.

'Now, let's get down to the fingerprints on the manuscript,' I said in a business-like tone. 'What have you discovered?'

'Not much, Sir,' Blundell said, clearly relieved to have reached another topic of conversation. 'One set were Fr Abbot's, made, presumably, when he handled the manuscript preparatory to giving it to you for the sale. One set is virtually illegible. And a third set belong to an unknown individual, at a guess the professor's. If it's Audrey's, it's too late now for confirmation. I suppose it could be Brother Denis's. Do you wish me to pursue that one?'

'No, the information won't do us much good. Unless it's someone with a criminal record, we're not going to find out anyway, unless we fingerprint every person connected with the case: the fair Elspeth, Angelo Costardu, all the monks, the professor, Mrs Professor, the auctioneers … We might end up doing it, but I think not for the moment. No, wait a minute, you'd better check up at least on our chief suspects: Angelo and Brother Jude. No, that won't do either. Jude could always give us a perfectly plausible reason for handling the manuscript; but go for our Sardinian friend. If it's his fingerprints we're looking at, I'd like to know how they got there. Now, moving on, did you ask the abbot about other visitors to the abbey who asked to see the manuscript?'

'I did, Sir. I gave him a ring yesterday morning, and he phoned me back yesterday afternoon. I had asked him to check back ten years, if that was possible, and he told me he thought it was possible. His answer was, None: not a single visitor, either in his own time or in that of his predecessor, Father Mark. Plenty of visitors, of course: monks' relations who travelled a long distance, occasional people to make a retreat, visiting monks, the abbot of Mount St Bernard's and so on, but not one person to see the Hermann manuscript.'

'That's strange,' I said, 'very strange. The only person we know of to have seen the manuscript is the professor, and why would he steal his own manuscript? So, despite what my friend Doctor Nibeaudaud asserted, it looks as if the thief had stolen what he had never seen, or had stolen it on the part of someone else who had never seen it either. I don't like this one bit. And did you get anywhere with finding out whether Audrey and the professor could have known each other?'

'No, Sir, not really, haven't had the time. But I'll pursue it, Sir, you can rely on me.'

'Well, don't bother. It was only a long shot, and from what Elspeth was saying at lunch, it's dead in the water.'

'I hope you don't mind my commenting, Sir?' Blundell asked in a non-committal sort of voice.

'No, of course not', I said. 'Why should I?'

'Well, Sir, what if we've been inventing a serious crime here where there isn't one?'

'What do you mean?' I asked.

'Well, we know that Jadwiga Zawadzki was stabbed in a street brawl. That had nothing to do with Our Lady of the Snows, the Hermann manuscript or anything else that we've been investigating. Now let us suppose that Professor Dodsworth is simply mistaken in his reading of the manuscript, and that what he bought at auction is the original: there was, and never has been, a copy or a forgery. It follows, therefore, that there was no theft from the monastery. Audrey Fletcher does a disappearing act at the monastery for reasons of her own. She starts a new life for herself in Birmingham, under an assumed name, but unfortunately she is the victim of a hit-and-run driver in a random accident. Could happen to anyone. Audrey is innocent of theft. Dodsworth is guilty of nothing more than overweening self-importance. What's left?'

'I'll tell you what's left, Sergeant: the anonymous phone-call to the abbot demanding that the abbey sell the Hermann manuscript, that's what!'

'Yes, I see that, Sir. Presumably whoever buried Jadwiga's body at the abbey made the phone-call. However, the abbey need not have surrendered quite so easily, and we're left with a bit of a prank: burying a body decently but in the wrong cemetery, followed by an idle threat.'

I considered this little speech for a few moments.

'Ye-e-es,' I said slowly. 'I can't help feeling that there's more to it than that, though. For example, is it just a coincidence that Jadwiga and Audrey resembled each other so closely that the one could be mistaken for the other? Do you really think that Professor Dodsworth could be so vociferous and positive unless he were quite certain of his ground? And I just don't trust Costardu.'

'No, Sir, but what if all he's guilty of is burying Jadwiga? Hardly a major crime shaking our society to its foundations!'

'And I don't trust Brother Jude, either,' I said, getting a bit exasperated.

'That's just his manner, Sir. Perhaps he'd been disobeying the monastic rules and feels uncomfortable about it.'

'There's something much more plausible than that, Sergeant, and that is that Brother Jude was responsible for the blackmailing phone-call to the abbot. His conscience smote him that the abbey was nursing the Hermann manuscript for no good reason, and he felt it his duty to pressurise the abbey into selling it for charity. He voted against the measure in chapter simply to obviate any suspicion, certain that the measure would be passed with a majority without his help.'

'Then you agree with me, Sir, that there is no serious crime?'

'Well, blackmail is a serious crime, even when committed against oneself.'

'But in that case Brother Jude would have to have known about the body in the cemetery, which was the lever the blackmailer used to pressurise the abbey into selling the manuscript.'

'Well, perhaps he was a witness. Perhaps he was staring out of the dorter window, idly watching the world go by, and happened to see the goings-on in the graveyard.'

'At dead of night? And the murder weapon? How did he know about that?'

'I'll think of something! And your own theory just doesn't seem to tie everything in together: Audrey's disappearance, her death, Jadwiga's burial at the abbey, the auction, the claim that the manuscript is a forgery. You're proposing a startling series of coincidences, if you don't mind my saying so!'

We appeared to be at a dead-end, despite all our inquiries and all the progress we had undoubtedly made; and yet again, when the professor's call came through, I felt I was not so much in charge of events as their victim.

Thirteen

Later that afternoon, Blundell came in to tell me that Angelo Costardu had, reluctantly, agreed to have his fingerprints taken so that he could be eliminated from the inquiry, and he had been duly eliminated – yet another line of investigation explored and found wanting! If his fingerprints – 'dabs' in the picturesque argot of the criminal classes – had been plastered over the manuscript, I should have excoriated him for risking damage to a precious mediaeval manuscript but also concluded that his carelessness deserved to lead to his exposure! There was, however, no evidence that he had been within a gnat's crotchet of the manuscript. This was a pity.

The professor's phone-call the following morning was to me personally, and I felt constrained, by a number of reasons, to deal with it personally rather than, as was my first reaction, to give it to uniform. For a start, the professor appealed to me, and it might have appeared churlish to hand him over to those who would normally have dealt with the matter. Secondly, it boosted my self-confidence to think that, even after the halting and so far fruitless progress made to recover the original Hermann manuscript, he still had enough faith in me to telephone me. And thirdly, I suppose that somewhere deep inside me I had hopes – vague and ill-formed but none the less hopes – that any new development, however humdrum and unpromising, might be the breakthrough I needed.

'Inspector Wickfield?' the well-known voice inquired.

'Yes, Professor. How are you?'

'I'm at my wits' end, Inspector, that's how I am. I wish to report a break-in at my house. The manuscript has been stolen!'

'Good heavens!' was all I could think to say in immediate reply. So not a break-through at all, but a break-in. Then carefully marshalling my thoughts, I added, 'Please tell me what happened'.

'My wife came down first thing this morning to find the kitchen door swinging open. A burglar has gone through into my study, broken into the safe and walked off with the Hermann manuscript. Would you believe it? I'm still numb with the shock.'

Could I face the eighty-five-mile journey again? I supposed I should have to.

'All right, Professor. I'll come over. I shall be with you in a couple of hours.' I phoned the local police-station to request that a constable meet me on the spot and to explain why I was asking them to let me in on the case. As I drove over, I was asking myself why the professor was so exercised about a manuscript which by his own admission was a fake and so, well, not quite worthless, but probably not worth a great deal. Why did its theft matter so much to him?

I drove up the familiar drive, again admiring the proportions and symmetry of the house and the warm colour of the red brick, the generous chimneys and the mullioned windows. The handsome front-door was studded and imposing. If I had become a university professor instead of a policeman, which feat would have required a completely different set of brain cells, I too could be enjoying, perhaps, such elegance and time-honoured charm. I should probably, also, have been just as useful to my fellow humans.

The professor was undoubtedly agitated.

'I'm so glad you've come, Inspector. I wouldn't trust the local constabulary with this one. Much too important.'

'Professor, a copy of a valuable manuscript has gone astray. It's probably not worth very much, if you don't my saying so.'

'Inspector, you clearly don't understand the situation at all. That copy is the only thing I have which will get me my money back.'

'Get you your money back? Would you explain, Professor?'

'You know as well as I do that I was sold a pup. You asked me to hold off before I took any action in the matter. Well, I didn't. I approached the auctioneers and told them that they owed me £11,500, because they knowingly sold me a fake. Do you know what they said?'

'I can guess. They said that the sale catalogue made no claims concerning the provenance or genuineness of the manuscript, that bidders bid on the principle of *caveat emptor*, and that they declined to reimburse you. Am I right?'

'Yes, in every detail.'

'So what do you propose now?'

'I propose to go back to the abbey and request that they approach the charity to which they negligently gave the proceeds. I'll have to get my money back that way.'

'And why is the stolen parchment so important?'

'Let me explain again, Inspector, since you seem to have forgotten the content of a previous conversation. The original manuscript had a quilisma on the seventeenth syllable of the text. What I bought at auction had not. In the easy version of the anthem, there is, of course, no quilisma: just too difficult for choirs that are not highly skilled. In the more difficult version, however, as composed by Hermann the Cripple, there is one, and later copies of the anthem faithfully reproduce it. How can I now prove to the abbot that my copy is a fake if I can't produce it? It's a disaster, there's no other word. Not only haven't I got the original manuscript, but I haven't got my money either. The abbey knows more than it is letting on, and I have to say, Inspector, that you are not blameless either.'

I stared at him.

'If you had allowed me to approach the abbey immediately, the thief wouldn't have had a chance to pinch it out of my safe.'

'Very well, Professor, let us not argue about that now. Would you be kind enough to show me and the constable the kitchen door and the safe?'

All this time we had been standing in the hall, a large panelled room smelling of cut flowers and apple-wood from the fire: gracious, very gracious, but not conducive, purely as standing-space, to the solution of the crime. The professor led us through a door at the back of the hall into the large and comfortable kitchen, where Mrs Dodsworth was preparing (I took it) the couple's midday meal. The back-door was closed, but a small pane of glass had a circle cut out of it to allow the passage of a burglarious arm and the twisting of the key. A neat, clearly professional, job. We returned to the hall, with apologies to Mrs Dodsworth (who was looking horsier than ever, may the heavens forgive me) for the disturbance, and went through another door into the study, with which I was already acquainted. The safe stood in the corner, where I had seen it before. The combination had been worked out by the burglar – no need for noisy explosives - and when the professor came down in the morning, the safe-door stood open, and the polished box which contained the parchment was missing: nothing else, just the copy of the Hermann manuscript. The burglar had retreated the way he had come. The constable assured me that he would mobilise the local team to take possible finger-prints, although neither of us expected so professional an operator to have left behind him – or her – such readable evidence, and that the station would check other burglaries in the vicinity to see whether this one could not be attributed to a known suspect.

When the constable had departed, with a promise to return early in the afternoon, I asked Professor Dodsworth whether he had any idea who might have taken his manuscript.

'Well, you see, Inspector, no one but myself and the official at the auction house to whom I spoke – and you, of course - knew that my manuscript was a fake. Everyone else would have imagined that I had bought the original and probably kept it in my safe at home. Of course, since the auction, all the world and his wife knew who had bought the item and how much he had paid and therefore how valuable it is. They would have had little difficulty in finding out where I lived: I am not totally unknown, you see, Inspector.'

'No, no, quite,' I hastened to comment.

'So really anyone could have had a go. The manuscript is extremely well-known at the moment, but ten or twenty years hence, the thief might stand a bit of a chance of palming it off on some unsuspecting, or unscrupulous, collector. My bet is on some international art-thief who hired a professional safe-breaker to rob me of my unique treasure. The fact that it is in reality a copy doesn't lessen the blow for me. You do see that now, don't you, Inspector?'

I took my leave of the professor and his woes and returned to Warwick full of surmises and suspicions. Whole new perspectives opened up before me, in such profusion that my poor mind was in a whirl. It was mid-afternoon when I re-entered the station, and Blundell had been assigned to another case in my absence. It did not matter greatly, as it gave me a little more time to organise my thoughts.

When we did meet in the morning, I had drawn up a table – I was for ever drawing up tables: the sign of a tidy, methodical and superior mind, I kept telling myself – to assist the ideational processes, and this is what I had decided to use as a basis of our discussion. I divided our data into facts and imponderables (or ambiguities, uncertainties), thus. (I should perhaps add, to forestall your objections, that I am fully aware that there is, philosophically, no such thing as a fact, if by 'fact' you mean a bare datum 'out there', since all data are filtered through our mental frames and so take on preconceived qualities. But am I, or are you, telling this story?)

facts

1. Audrey Fletcher did a disappearing act.
2. Jadwiga Zawadzki was buried in the abbey cemetery.
3. A male voice phoned the abbot and told him to put the Hermann manuscript up for sale.
4. The abbey no longer possessed either the Hermann manuscript itself or a copy of it. (I admit I was not very sure about this one.)

ambiguities

1. Audrey Fletcher was killed – deliberately or by accident?
2. The Hermann manuscript exists in the original and in a copy, or one or the other of these.
3. We are not getting the truth from Brother Jude, Angelo Costardu or the professor.

4. Either the original manuscript or a copy was burgled from the professor's house in Lincoln – or perhaps neither.

You will appreciate that I was beginning to doubt everyone's story, except that of the abbot, who must surely be above suspicion – mustn't he? This was also why I told Blundell, when he came in for the conference, that the professor's account of the burglary – that an international ring, or perhaps a criminal individual, was taking advantage of the recent publicity surrounding the Hermann manuscript - although it was perfectly feasible, did not convince me. This case was, if you will pardon the colloquialism, squidgy from the start: when one squeezed in one place, it bulged in another, and one never got to the end of the squeezing and the bulging. I was therefore inclined to believe that the burglary at the professor's house was part of the original plot and not an independent heist on the part of individuals whom we had not yet encountered in the case. At the same time, I would bear the possibility in mind. I should perhaps have done better to convene in a public house over lunch, but I was anxious to hold our conference sooner rather than later, and nine o'clock in the morning is no hour to be imbibing in public – even if we could have found a place open to receive us. I had therefore organised coffee – a couple of mugs brewed on the ring in the office – and biscuits – a packet produced from my drawer. We were ready.

I filled Blundell in on my visit to Lincoln, gave him a few minutes to digest the information, and then invited him to come up with a hypothesis. If the burglary was genuine, had the original manuscript been taken or only a copy? And who was behind it? And what if the burglary were staged by the professor himself, for his own devious purposes? Teasing questions!

'Well, Sir, our villains, or I should say suspected villains, are Audrey, who has passed to her eternal reward, Mr Costardu, Brother Jude and the professor. Of course there may be others, of whom yet we have no cognisance.'

'You mean we don't know about them yet?'

'Yes, Sir, that's what I said. I ask myself in turn which of them benefited from the burglary.'

'This is very good, Sergeant. Carry on.'

'First, our Sardinian friend Angelo. We suspect him of being Audrey's accomplice in picking up Jadwiga's body and burying it. He can't be the voice behind the blackmail phone-call, because his accent, although slight, is still noticeable. If the burial was designed to trigger the sale of the manuscript, he hoped that his reward for assistance would be a share of the proceeds of the sale. He was thwarted in this by the action of the mystery voice, who shunted the proceeds towards a charity. The mystery voice and Angelo therefore had opposing interests. Because in the first round the mystery voice won, Angelo took his revenge by stealing the manuscript from the professor, believing it to be the original, and hoping to flog it for a vast sum. How's that, Sir?'

'Good, Sergeant, very good. Two slight drawbacks, neither of them insurmountable. Firstly, does Angelo have the skills needed to house-break and safe-break? Secondly, if she and Angelo were in the affair together, why were they not together when she lived as Jayne Templeton? Go on, Sergeant.'

'Secondly, then, Sir, Brother Jude. We know he voted against the abbey's sale of the manuscript. Perhaps, as you suggested earlier, this was bluff, but perhaps he had a genuine reason. What if he knew the manuscript was only a copy, because he was responsible for it? Any sale would subject it to close scrutiny, and its inauthenticity could have been discovered. Now of course he couldn't have burgled the professor's residence himself, but he could have arranged with a friend to do so, improbable though that sounds. This was to prevent the professor from making any capital out of the fake manuscript, at the abbey's expense. I reckon that in this case, Brother Denis has the original manuscript in his possession, safely concealed in his cell, say, so that the abbey cannot, simply cannot, commit the unforgivable crime of flogging the precious manuscript, in whatever cause, worthy or not.'

'Good, Sergeant. That coheres admirably with the fact that Brother Jude studied the art of illumination with Brother Denis, as he admitted. They were of one mind, let us say, in keeping the manuscript in the abbey. Brother Denis secretes the original and makes a perfect copy to hide his act.'

'So what's wrong with that suggestion, Sir?' How well he was getting to know my methods!

'Well, it doesn't go any way to explaining the phone-call and the sad burial, does it? Brother Denis has been out of the action for years, by all accounts, and I can't see Brother Jude on his own picking a stray body up in Warwick, burying it, and then triggering an auction of the manuscript to which he was so attached by making a blackmailing call to his own abbot. So go on to the professor.'

'Yes, Sir. The professor has lost the manuscript and his money – if, that is, he was palmed off with a copy and is not spinning us a tale. Realising that neither the auction-house nor the abbey is going to reimburse him, he stages a burglary in his own house to claim off the insurance.'

'There is a serious objection to that, Sergeant, and I suspect you know what it is.'

'Yes, Sir, you are going to say that he couldn't claim off the insurance because he had already told us his manuscript was a fake. The insurers are going to offer very little, if anything, for a copy worth a few bob. Of course, he might have hoped to get away with it, thinking that the insurers and the police are hardly likely to put their heads together. So he tells the police he's got a fake, and he then changes tack and tells the insurers he's been robbed of the original. The objection to that is, of course, that he called you into investigating the burglary. For my idea to work, he would have needed to keep quiet.'

'I congratulate you, Sergeant, on a game effort. I'm not sure I can do any better myself, but what about this? Because none of your reconstructions seems to work very well *on its own*, let's build on them by combining them. Let's say, for example, that the whole affair is initiated by Brother Jude, not a maverick but a deeply committed Christian anxious to extend the abbey's influence in charitable affairs. He knows, through Brother Denis, that the abbey has a copy of its most famous possession which is indistinguishable from the original. He thinks up a scheme whereby the copy is sold to raise a lot of money for charity. On one occasion when his sister visits him, he raises the issue with her. Could she manage to think of a scheme whereby the abbey is obliged to put the manuscript up for sale? In cooperation with Brother Denis, or knowing that Brother Denis has the original safely guarded in his room, he substitutes for it in the box the careful copy, and then waits for Audrey to come up with some scheme. Audrey sees a body in the street and goes in with

Angelo to bury it at the abbey. Her scheme to disappear arises entirely out of the fortuitous similarity between the body they come across and herself, and her decision to effect the scheme is taken on the spur of the moment. Brother Jude knows nothing of any of this. The first he knows is of the body's discovery and the subsequent chapter-meeting at which the sale of the manuscript is canvassed. This takes care of all the "facts" listed above except the last one. It means that if we search Brother Denis' room, or wherever else Brother Jude indicates, we shall unearth the Hermann manuscript in all its pristine glory – minus the box, of course. Of the ambiguities, it takes care of 1. (accident), 2. (both), 3. (no, we're not) and 4. (the copy). The only murder therefore is that of poor Jadwiga, and Brother Jude is guilty of, I suppose one should call it blackmail, but for the worthiest motives. Audrey and Angelo were his pawns. On the other hand, one could argue that he is guilty of gross dishonesty by proposing to sell as an original work what he knows to be only a copy. Does Brother Jude strike you as dishonest to that extent? Perhaps he does!

'Now, however, let's start at a different place. Let's start with the professor. He has long desired to get his grubby, sticky little hands on the Hermann manuscript, for his own delectation. His trouble is that the abbey has no intention of selling. He therefore contacts an acquaintance, Audrey Fletcher, and says, Well, my dear, what about it? If you can persuade the abbey to sell the manuscript, I'll slip you £500 for your trouble. She does so, and he buys the manuscript. Things then go awry, because he realises he's been had for a sucker: Audrey and Jude see to it that they get the original, while all the professor gets is a measly copy. He can't get his hands on Audrey to throttle the life out of her, because she's done a bunk, but he can get his own back on Jude by suing the abbey. He knows that, rather than admit they have knowingly put a copy up for sale, they will sell other assets in order to give him his money back and keep him quiet. He knows he will never now own the Hermann manuscript, but at least he's put the abbey to a double loss: the proceeds of the auction to a charity, and the same again to him to reimburse him. It was he who made the blackmail phone-call, because he thought the monks were more likely to agree to put the manuscript up for sale if the money was going to a charity than if they were keeping it for themselves. This reconstruction takes care of facts 1. and 2., as with

Brother Jude above. Fact no.4 he doesn't care about, because he knows he'll never get the original. As regards the ambiguities, Audrey died by accident, the Hermann manuscript certainly exists in copy – the rest is immaterial to him, and he has told us some of the truth but not all of it.

'Let's try once more, this time taking the swarthy and suspicious Angelo as our villain. He gets to hear, through Audrey, of a valuable manuscript lurking in the abbey scriptorium. He determines that he shall be the possessor of it, so that he can flog it on the black market and net himself a few thousand quid. He and Audrey, driving through Warwick one evening in a nonchalant sort of way, spy a dead body and purloin it. Burying it in the monastic cemetery is their way of putting pressure on the abbey to bring the Hermann manuscript into the open: otherwise Angelo hasn't a hope of knowing where it is. He attends the auction, learns the address of the purchaser, and then steals it from him. Unknown to him, he is stealing not the original, which Brothers Denis and Jude have conspired to hide away, but a copy, but that doesn't bother him. When the moment is ripe, he will slip back to Sardinia and dispose of it through his bandit friends.'

'So who made the phone-call?' asked Blundell.

'I don't know. Perhaps an English friend of his, for a small consideration.'

'And Audrey?'

'Oh, she gets cold feet, does a bunk and then threatens to expose him. She has to be silenced, so, sucking up to Elspeth, he discovers her present whereabouts, runs her down, and carries on as if nothing had happened, biding his time. He has told us a pack of lies, but this theory covers all the facts and answers the ambiguities, making him out to be a particularly nasty piece of work. But at least it lets Jude and the amiable professor off the hook. In any case, they can't all be villains – can they?' I added hopelessly.

I shall not bother you with details of our further conversation: that would be to strain your patience beyond endurance. Suffice it to say that we attempted a number of other reconstructions, none of them any more successful or less open to objection. The more our ideas swirled round the facts, the more convinced I became that we were approaching the truth, if only we could fasten on the inalienable core. There was nothing for it, I decided, but to interview yet again our three main suspects and squeeze and squeeze until we got the truth. Sooner or later, one of them would slip up, and that would be our chance. So far, we had only surmise to lay before a panel of twelve good and true citizens, and if, as Blundell had mooted, there should prove to be no serious crime, I could at least close the case and receive the DCI's warm congratulations.

Fourteen

Kindly Reader, you have persevered thus far, and you will have appreciated how confusing our task was. I wish to give you now an account of our interviews with the three main suspects, and I invite you to judge, as we had to, where the truth lay and where, on the contrary, our path was strewn with lies and half-truths. I wonder whether you will come to the same conclusions as we did.

I thought we should begin with Brother Jude. There was no particular reason for this, other than the considerations that the affair started at the abbey and that Brother Jude could, if he so chose, and other things being equal (which I realised they were not), provide us with the essential information concerning the role that Brother Denis might have played in our drama. Although I desired maximum solemnity, to inspire our interviewee with the gravity of the situation, I considered that visiting him at the abbey was more seemly than instructing the abbot to release him for questioning at the station. It was in the first days of December, therefore, that Blundell, as amanuensis, *aide-de-camp* and general dog's-body, and I drove out to Our Lady of the Snows. It was an overcast and drizzly day, not one to instil feelings of hope and success in jaded breasts. We turned off on to the Baginton road at Ashow and motored gently up the valley, the only moving thing, apart from a few cows, in sight. Our thoughts – I presume to include my sergeant, who was the driver, in this pronoun – were occupied with the case in general and with the coming interview in particular. I must tell you, however, at the risk of contradicting myself, that the abbey buildings were as soothing and picturesque as ever, even against a backdrop of bare trees and sodden undergrowth. The lane is nearly straight, but the hedges and trees mean that, from the south, the visitor perceives the abbey piecemeal, a tower here, a turret there, poking up amongst the stripped branches and the dull foliage. Then to the visitor turning into the drive the buildings present themselves in their full architectural excellence. We parked in front of the gatehouse and prepared to do battle.

Again I was struck by the contrast between Brother Jude's somewhat rugged and stiff appearance – stocky build, heavy features, bull-neck, cropped hair – and the pleasant modulation of his educated voice. He seemed quite at ease. In the Blue Parlour, four arm-chairs were as usual positioned round a central coffee-table, two of the chairs having their backs to the unlit fireplace, and the three of us therefore necessarily occupied three corners of the square thus provided. Blundell and I had agreed – that is to say, I had proposed and Blundell had sensibly seconded me – that we confront the suspect with our suspicions, with little preamble. I promptly reneged on our agreement; but then, as the elder by six years, that was my prerogative.

'Brother Jude,' I began in the classic and elegant style that I have made my own in the course of numerous investigations since this first one, 'Father Abbot will have told you why we are here. We are not satisfied that all those connected with your sister's disappearance and then untimely death have been telling us the truth. We wish you, therefore, to be entirely clear in your mind that no prevarication will do. There are unpleasant consequences for those who waste police time, seek to obstruct the course of justice or hide facts material to a murder investigation. We therefore require from you, here and now, the truth and only the truth. I hope I make myself plain?'

Jude nodded his head but said nothing. His calm demeanour had not altered. Blundell had begun scribbling.

'Now I know that you are not familiar with all the actors in the drama or all aspects of the case, but what you are going to tell us is neither more nor less than *all* you know, from your own perspective. May I start by asking how you came to join Our Lady of the Snows?' This was a psychological ploy designed to set the young monk at his ease. That is about as far as my psychology goes. Brother Jude weighed the question.

'Gentlemen, there is no secret about that. We were a practising Catholic family, and our parents had brought us up to be God-fearing, devout Christians whose contribution to the world was to be positive and creative. As I went through school, the idea finally crystallised of becoming a monk, or perhaps a friar, and I made a few inquiries: the Jesuits, the Holy Ghost Fathers and the Christian Brothers in particular. What put me off all of these, admirable religious congregations though they are, is that, for me, insufficient time is left for meditation, contemplation, prayer: aspects of the religious life that many mistakenly declare to be less active modes of charity. So I looked at a couple of contemplative orders and came up with the Gilbertines. I suppose I should rephrase that: the Gilbertines came up with me. You see, Inspector, if you go along with Gireaudoux's definition of destiny as "the relentless logic of each day we live", the Gilbertines, with their local connections and their semi-Benedictine rule, seemed to be reaching out for me.'

'But you were not born in Warwickshire,' I interrupted.

'No, I wasn't, but, by divine Providence, we moved, just as I was finalising my aspirations, to within ten miles of a small, quiet monastery which I thought would suit me to perfection. So I joined.'

I did some rapid calculations.

'That leaves nine or ten years between your leaving school and your joining the Gilbertines,' I said. 'What did you do in those years?'

'Well, Inspector, from school I went to art college - '

'In Newcastle?' I asked.

'Yes, but how did you know, Inspector?'

'Oh, it doesn't matter, please continue.'

' - and I got a job as a draughtsman with an engineering firm in Carlisle.'

'Did you enjoy it?'

'Yes, I did. I felt I was being useful.'

'Did you ever consider marriage, or is that too personal a question?'

'No, I don't mind answering that. I considered marriage, but by this time the attraction of the religious life was becoming more and more insistent. In any case, I had never managed to meet Miss Right.'

'What I don't understand is that, if you were settled in Carlisle, why did you up sticks when your parents and sisters moved to Warwick?'

'That's not an easy one to answer, Inspector. I suppose I felt rather unsettled by the, er, events which led to my parents' move – '

'Yes, Brother, Elspeth has told us about them.'

'Oh, I see. So I thought I should have a change of scenery myself. I had hardly got a job in Warwick when I decided to approach the abbot of Our Lady of the Snows. The rest you know.'

'Have you ever regretted that step?'

'No, never.'

'You're content in the monastery?'

'Yes, completely. I couldn't ask for a better life.'

That all seemed fairly reasonable and above board, even to my sceptical mind, so I proceeded to less general matters.

'Now, Brother, you have told us what happened when your sister Audrey visited you on the 4 June this year. Do you stand by your account?'

'Yes, of course, Inspector. You don't think I told you lies, do you? Why should I do that?'

'OK, Brother, we'll pass on. I want to ask you again about the Hermann manuscript. My sergeant here' – and I waived a proprietorial hand in Blundell's direction – 'told me that you claimed to know nothing about a copy of the Hermann manuscript. Is that true?'

'Yes, certainly, Inspector.'

'Had you ever seen the Hermann manuscript?'

'Yes.'

'In what circumstances?'

'Brother Denis showed it me one afternoon. I remember discussing the techniques of it with him.'

'Did he say anything about its importance or value?'

'Yes, he said that in his opinion it was the abbey's single most precious artefact.'

'Did he seem knowledgeable about it?'

'He did. He told me he had undertaken a little research about Hermann and about the history of the *Alma Redemptoris Mater* in particular, and that he had acquired a huge devotion to the badly crippled monk. He always referred to him as "the blessed Hermann".'

'And you're absolutely certain he never mentioned a copy?'

'Oh, but he did!'

'But you told my sergeant that he had never made a copy.'

'Yes, I did, but I meant exactly what I said, that Brother Denis had never made one. I didn't say he had never mentioned it.'

'Please explain yourself.'

'Brother Denis was well-known for his exquisite copies of other mediaeval manuscripts in the abbey's possession. When I asked him about the Hermann manuscript, he said he would never attempt it. The original was too sacred and it was perfect: it should never have an equal.'

'You saw the original: on more than one occasion?'

'No, only the once.'

'Can you remember whether it carried a quilisma on the *ma- of manes* in the second line?'

'No, sorry, Inspector. No idea. I didn't note the music as closely as that.'

'If Brother Denis *had* made a copy, where would he have kept it, do you think?'

'Oh, but I've just told you. I am absolutely certain he never made a copy.'

'Could anyone else have made one?'

'Well, yes, I suppose so, but in my time at the abbey, no one else has ever demonstrated the skills of Brother Denis. None of the monks I have known could have brought it off.'

'Right, Brother, could I now come to the chapter at which it was decided to sell the Hermann manuscript.'

'Yes, Inspector.' No trace of unease here.

'I was present, as you may remember, and I remarked at the time that you had voted against a sale. May I ask why?'

'I should have thought it was obvious, Inspector. Here was the abbey's most precious possession, and it was proposed to hawk it for worldly gain.'

'But the proceeds of any sale were to go to a charity,' I countered.

'Yes, they were, which made the whole thing worse.'

'What do you mean?' Poor Blundell was scribbling away all this time, desperately trying to capture the cut and thrust of the conversation as it developed under my skilful handling.

'To sell treasures to aid the poor is a way of confessing that prayer on its own is insufficient. That's a travesty of the monastic way of life, as far as I am concerned.'

'So why didn't you speak up at the meeting?'

'Because others had already expressed my views.'

'Were you upset to have lost the vote?'

'Yes, of course. I felt that the chapter had made a bad mistake, for which posterity would never forgive us.'

'Have you forgiven those who voted in favour of selling?'

'Yes, of course, Inspector, it is what we are enjoined to do by our religion.'

'No ill-feeling?'

'None – I hope.'

'Would it ever occur to you to try to regain the manuscript for the abbey?'

'I don't see how that could be done, Inspector. The only possibility is that the buyer should gift it back to the abbey, but that was not going to happen, and in fact it has not happened.'

'One final thing, Brother, if I may. Did you ever talk to your sister Audrey about the manuscript?'

'Possibly. It wasn't a secret, you know.'

'Did you ever show it to her?'

'No, definitely not. You see, I would never have taken it out of the scriptorium, and she was not allowed into that part of the abbey.'

'Would she have known that it was valuable?'

'Yes, probably, but I don't see what that's got to do with anything.'

So our interview ended. His story was a far cry, a very far cry, from my reconstruction that had him at the centre of a web of intrigue. Was his defence, his protestation of ignorance, convincing? Only time was to tell.

Our next port of call was Lincoln police-station, where Professor Dodsworth had been invited to attend for interview.

'This is outrageous, Inspector, to be summoned to the station as if I were some common felon, some sort of social pariah to be moved about at will.'

'Professor, Professor,' I said soothingly, 'coming to the station is standard procedure. It says nothing about your status in society or before the law. It is a simple measure designed to mark the official character of this conversation.   After all, we are investigating a serious crime – a series of serious crimes - and we wish to treat them seriously, don't we?'

'Humph,' was all I got.

The three of us were seated in one of the station interview-rooms: not, I admit, the cosiest apartment which it had ever been my pleasure to inhabit, but on the other hand it was not nearly so forbidding as some I have seen. It was a smallish room, perhaps twelve by twelve, simply but decently furnished with a table and three chairs, curtains, a couple of framed pictures and a water jug. I had also requested a pot of tea and some biscuits, which arrived in due course. The professor was dressed much as I had seen him at home on the occasion of our previous meeting, but he naturally appeared much less relaxed in an environment not of his own making.

'Professor' – I adopted my formal voice, hoping to impress this tetchy and self-important man with my authority – 'you will forgive me, I hope, for saying that we are not convinced we have yet got to the bottom of this affair or of your part in it.'

I paused forcefully. A difficult man to deal with, the professor.

'By your own admission, you approached the auctioneers to demand that you be reimbursed.'

'Certainly.'

'But you got no joy, because you bought the manuscript that had been on view in the auction-room beforehand.'

'Yes.'

'You hadn't spotted then that it was a fake?'

'No, it never occurred to me to go through it note by note. I wasn't to know that a single quilisma would betray its inauthenticity. As I told you, it was only at the monks' performance a fortnight later that I cottoned on.'

'And you didn't realise that the auctioneers would have covered themselves?'

'It was worth a try.'

'Did you tell them it was a fake?'

'Not in as many words: they would have laughed in my face. I told them this was not the manuscript in the possession of Our Lady of the Snows and that therefore its provenance could not be vouched for. I bought in good faith, believing what I bought to be the work of Hermannus Constrictus, whom I admire very much. I charged the auction-house with false representation, because they made claims which turned out to be at best misleading, at worst fraudulent.'

'Having failed in your objective with Chapman and Thomas, your next intention was to approach the abbot of Our Lady of the Snows?'

'Yes, I certainly intended to pursue all possible paths.'

'In what way could they be thought to be responsible?'

'It occurred to me that they had deliberately substituted the copy for the original. Somebody must have done. I'm not blaming the abbot himself, but he must ultimately bear responsibility for the deception.'

'Let me put you a question, Professor, which is not at all meant to be offensive. Could you be mistaken in your estimation of the status of your manuscript?'

I thought he was going to explode. His cheeks swelled, his eyes hardened, he clenched his fists, his chest heaved.

'Mistaken? Me, mistaken? How dare you?'

Ignoring this petty display of temper, I ploughed on.

'You told me you spent a year at Westvleteren Abbey when you were young. Have I got that right?'

'Yes.'

'Would a year give you enough time to acquire the basics of illumination?'

'I'm not sure I see what you're driving at, Inspector. It might have done, but Westvleteren has no tradition of it. The monks never bothered with mediaeval manuscripts, that I know of.'

'What car do your run, Professor?'

'Car? Car? What's that got to do with anything?'

'Just answer my question, please, Professor.'

'I've got a Humber, an old one. It's standing in the garage now, and you can phone my wife to check. You have a hell of an impertinence, Inspector, if I may say so.'

'Professor, I mean no offence. I must establish the truth of all aspects of this case, you must see that. How long have you had the car?'

'Five years, maybe a bit more.'

'Thank you. Now the local police have investigated your break-in, and they compliment the burglar on his skill.'

'What's that supposed to mean?'

'It means simply that so little damage was done, they wonder whether you could be responsible for it yourself.'

The professor's eyes started from his head. He half-rose from his seat, and I wondered for an instant whether violence would be perpetrated.

'Inspector, that is beyond the pale. I demand to see the station superintendent immediately.'

'Professor, you have no grounds for complaint. I am putting certain questions to you, you are asked to give a truthful response, that is all. If you are innocent, no harm is done, I hope. I have several other uncomfortable questions for you, but would you prefer me to wait until you are more composed?'

You will appreciate that I was feeling my way. I had never before conducted such an interview. My training before being promoted to the impressive heights of detective inspector allowed me to sit in on interviews conducted by others and to insert questions occasionally, but to be in charge of an investigation was a novel, and a not entirely pleasant, experience, and to conduct such an interview as that in which I was involved at that moment was entirely without precedent. I was determined to override all the professor's objections. His self-important manner had riled me, in a way that Brother Jude's quiet stolidity had not, and I was surprised by the difference in my own demeanour when faced with two such different subjects. I asked myself whether I was really in charge of the conversation or merely responding to stimuli from the other.

'My next question, Professor, is whether you had any prior acquaintance with the Fletcher family of Warwick?'

'I've never heard of them. I told you that.'

'Parents Belinda and Ronald, both deceased, children Jude, Oliver (deceased), Elspeth and Audrey: ring any bells?'

'No, no and no.'

'Jayne Templeton?'

'No.'

'Angelo Costardu?'

'Look, Inspector, what is this? I know none of these people. I've never heard of any of them. They're all complete strangers.'

'Where were you on the night of 4 November this year?'

'How should I know?'

'If you have your diary on you, I suggest you consult it,' I said, a shade acidly. He fumbled in his pocket, produced a diary in the final stages of decay – it was December, after all – and asked me to repeat the date.

'4 November,' I said. 'A young girl called Jayne Templeton was run down in the street and killed.'

He leafed through his diary. 'Meeting of the Lincolnshire Archaeological Society in the afternoon – I was delivering a paper, you know – and that's all. I suppose I was at home that evening, since there is no other entry.'

'What do you and your wife generally do in the evenings, Professor?'

'I don't see what business that is of yours. If you must know, we engage in intellectual pursuits like reading. Does that satisfy you?'

The conversation was getting a little difficult. I had antagonised him to a point where he was withdrawing any cooperation he may have offered at the beginning.

'One last question, then, Professor. May I just ask whether your university pension allows you to spend £11,500 on a single manuscript? Do you have other sources of income?'

I feared I had gone too far. He controlled himself, with an effort.

'It's none of your bloody business,' he expostulated at length, 'but if you must know, my parents left me well off – not wealthy, just comfortable. I can afford to indulge my little whims. Does that answer your question - Inspector?'

I was disappointed not to have forced the professor to incriminate himself in any way, but I felt I had been fair with him and to have asked all the questions that needed putting. In that sense, the interview was a success. I had strayed from my original script, turning over in my mind reconstructions other than the ones I had discussed with Blundell. I had one more interview to conduct, and I should then review my options. The professor had proved a broken reed, in that he offered no support to a conspiracy between him and any other character in the frame and denied any involvement in any action of an illegal nature, but my latest conversation with him might yet prove productive on further consideration.

Third on our list came Angelo, our *émigré* islander from the warmth of the Mediterranean. He was well wrapped up against the December cold. Of average height, he impressed with his muscley frame, broad shoulders and agile step. Black curls, untidy but fetching, framed a masculine face. He had a broad smile – not that we encouraged smiling. When we had convened at the Warwick station, I apologised for taking him out of his work but explained that needs must in a murder investigation. I also explained to him the necessity of entirely truthful answers to our questions.

'Mr Costardu, I'd like to start by asking you to tell us how it is that you now live in Warwick. Surely Sardinia is both warm and beautiful? Why move?'

'I've only visited the island once,' he said, 'when my grandmother died four years ago.'

'How did your parents, then, come to settle here?'

'The family lived in the north-east of the island, in a hill village not far from Arzachena. They still do. My father was a shepherd. Now, the whole area is beginning to be developed for tourists: villas, hotels, helicopter pads, golf-courses and so on – the stunning "Emerald Coast", you understand - but in those days there was little work and life was spoilt by banditry. Our small flock was always at risk; any help from the government – and Rome seemed a very long way away – was siphoned off by corrupt officials, and the future seemed bleak. Is this what you want to know, Inspector?' he said as he broke off.

'Yes, yes, please go on.'

'Eventually my father said that he would come to Britain and try for work. He would send money back and hope that the family could join him. In the end I was the only one who came over. My mother said she preferred to stay put; my elder brother moved to the north of Italy; my sister married a local guy, a butcher. My mother died a year or two after that, and also there never seemed to be enough money for my father and me to travel back to Sardinia. And then my father married an Italian woman he had met over here. So here I am, more or less British.'

'You work in a bacon factory, I understand.'

'Yes. The wages aren't good, but I survive.'

I remembered that Elspeth had described Angelo as a 'creepy, greasy type', but I did not find this myself. Could I, however, vouch for his honesty? I'm not sure.

'How did you meet Audrey Fletcher?' I asked.

'At a club.'

'Was the attraction immediate and mutual?'

'Yes, I think so. She was a very pretty girl, in her early twenties, not boisterous or flamboyant' – where had he picked that word up? – 'certainly quieter than her sister when I met Elspeth later. We got on fine from the start.'

'We know, Angelo, and you know that we know, that Audrey staged her own disappearance and went to live in Birmingham as Jayne Templeton. You do know that, of course?'

He nodded.

'Why did she do that?'

'She said she was coming into some money, enough to buy our own house, but she preferred to move away from Warwick in case people started asking questions.'

'Questions? Why should people ask questions?'

'I think she thought people would begin to wonder where the money came from. She didn't want people to "put two and two together", she said.'

'What did she mean by that, do you suppose?'

'Look, Inspector, I don't know. There was probably something a little underhand in how she was going to get this money. She never told me.'

'What did she tell you when she disappeared?'

'She said I was not to worry. We should need to separate for a few months, until things died down - '

'What "things"?'

'I don't know, Inspector,' he said in an exasperated voice. 'And the less I knew, the better, she said.'

'And then?'

'She gave me an address in Birmingham, and said I was to contact her only in a dire emergency. She would send for me when she was ready.'

'Now you are probably aware that a girl was picked up in a street in Warwick and buried at the monastery of Our Lady of the Snows. She was dressed in Audrey's clothes, and at first we took her to be Audrey. Do you know anything about that?'

'No, why should I?'

'Come on, Angelo, you were close to Audrey. You must have known what was happening.'

'I swear to you, Inspector, I knew nothing about it. All I know is that Audrey had a brother in the monastery. I have never been there, don't even know where it is. I had no idea a body dressed in Audrey's clothes had been found there.'

'Didn't Elspeth tell you?'

'Elspeth? Audrey had told me not to contact her. Everything

would work out between us, but I just had to be patient. In the meantime, I was to act as if she had died in mysterious circumstances, and I was not to try to get in touch with her brother or her sister. She said it was for the best.'

'Do you like Elspeth?'

'No, she's quite different from Audrey, much more aggressive, rather brassy. No, that's the wrong word, but if you know her, you'll know what I mean.'

'And did Audrey ever get in touch with you after her disappearance?'

'Yes, once, Inspector. I got a postcard from somewhere on the south coast, somewhere like Bournemouth, with just three kisses on it.'

'And you knew it was from her?'

'Of course. I had no other girl-friend.'

'And how did you come to hear of Audrey's death?'

'It was in the *Midland Gazette*.'

'I'm sorry to say I don't believe a word of what you're saying,' I told him after a pause. 'You want me to believe that you and Audrey intended to make a go of things and yet she never took you into her confidence? I think you knew about everything from the start. You knew she intended to disappear, how she was going to do it, you knew all about the girl's body – didn't you? You helped Audrey plant the body in the abbey cemetery. You also knew how Audrey was going to "come into her money" by stealing a valuable manuscript from the monastery. Look, Angelo, I want the truth, you're not giving it to me, and I'm going to get it.'

Angelo looked bewildered. 'Inspector, I've told you the truth.'

'Then all I can say is that Audrey didn't trust you very far. Do you call that love?'

This was not a very fair comment, and I regretted having uttered it. My intention was not to undermine Angelo's conviction in Audrey's regard for him, but somehow the remark slipped out. I was frustrated at getting so little information from my victim.

'Inspector, I know I'm not very bright. Audrey said that the less I knew, the less I should be worried by it. I could safely leave everything to her, she would see that all turned out well.'

'Have you ever met Professor Dodsworth?'

'No. I've never heard of him.'

'Have you got a car?'

'A car, on my wages? No, Inspector, no car.'

'Can you drive?'

'No. Look, Inspector, why are you asking me all these questions?'

'Where were you on the night of 4 November? It was a Friday.'

'I don't know.'

'Think!'

'That was the night Audrey was killed, wasn't it? You can't think I had anything to do with that! I loved her.'

Determined not to be baulked by his repeated denials, I steamed on.

'I'll tell you what I think, Costardu. I think you not only helped Audrey bury the girl's body in the abbey cemetery, but you got someone to phone the abbey with a spot of blackmail, you attended the auction of the precious manuscript, discovered who bought it and where he lived, and then you burgled his house to steal it.'

'Inspector, none of that is true, I swear it. Burgling? stealing? I don't know what you're talking about.'

I decided to go back to our original interview with the young Sardinian.

'You know what a scriptorium is?'

'Yes.'

'How do you know?'

'When I first got to know Audrey, she told me about her brother in the monastery and how one of his favourite places was the scriptorium. I asked her what it meant.'

'And what did she say?'

'She said it was where the monks copied manuscripts. Her brother was very keen to learn, apparently.'

'And you don't know where the scriptorium at Our Lady of the Snows is?'

'Inspector, I've told you, I don't even know where Our Lady of the Snows is.'

I left our conversation there. On our first meeting with him, both Blundell and I had come away with the impression that Angelo was on the defensive. That could be explained now by his awareness that something was afoot to which he was not a party.

Well, I have tried to give you a fair and accurate account of our three crucial interviews. The fact that Brother Jude and Angelo Costardu were more likeable characters than our friend the professor did not mean that they were telling the truth. Conversely, the fact the Professor Dodsworth was not very likeable at all did not mean that he was telling us lies. I had hoped to arrive at the truth, and in a way we did, but the truth lay outside the interviews, at the conclusion of threads of reasoning arising out of what we had been told:

And thus do we of wisdom and of reach,

With windlasses and with assays of bias,

By indirections find directions out.

You may be closer now than we were; in which case, you would have beaten us to unravelling the tangled skein.

Fifteen

At the time of these events, my wife Beth and I lived in a 1930s' semi-detached house on the outskirts of Leamington Spa. A small front garden, containing a few roses and a plum tree, separated us from the pavement. Behind the house was a large garden backing on to the gardens of the houses behind us. The entrance hall led to two reception rooms and the kitchen, while the stairs led to three bedrooms and a bathroom. Blenheim Palace it was not, but our salaries, even combined, were modest, we had two small boys, and we were saving hard. Furthermore, with our younger son only three, Beth had elected to give up work until he went to school.

I know exactly what you are thinking. Why is Wickfield giving me an account of his domestic arrangements? Does he imagine that they are of the slightest interest to me? Please be patient: all will be made clear (I hope). Just a little more, while I continue to set the scene. Do you wish, or do you not wish, after all this time, to learn why I have always thought of this case as *The Spider's Banquet*?

Where was I? Oh, yes, our house in Avonlea Rise. The front room we used sparingly, as a dining-room for more formal occasions: Easter and Christmas, for example, or when we entertained. The back room was the sitting-room: cosy, untidy, lived-in. French windows led into the garden. The coal fire had been replaced with a gas fire. There was a gramophone and a wireless, an upright piano, lots of books, and of course some comfortable chairs. A few poorly-tended pot-plants sat here and there. Pictures, mainly prints, adorned the walls: a reproduction Renoir, a Farquharson, a Turner (which I never liked: a gift from a great aunt – too many vague daubs).

That evening, Beth had put the boys to bed. We never had any trouble, and we delighted in their company, but still, evenings were best, for me at any rate, when there were just the two of us. No one in the police-force can guarantee to be home after tea, but I always regretted, and resented, being absent at that time of day. The evening wore on. I was reading *Kenilworth* for about the fourth time, but I put it down at the conclusion of a chapter and picked up the day's crossword.

After a while, I addressed my wife across the hearth-rug. '"Very cold", four letters. Any ideas? It's defeated me.' Beth looked up from her magazine. She thought.

'What about "dead"?' she said at length. I was speechless with admiration. 'Nice one,' I said feelingly.

'Shall I put a record on if you're only doing the crossword?' she asked.

'By all means,' I muttered. '"Bookmaker's secret arrangement secures advantage", nine letters, none yet in. I was struggling.

'What about a bit of Roussel?' she said as I bit the end of my pencil.

'Yes, fine,' I said absently.

'*The Spider's Banquet:* will that do?'

'What?' I almost shouted. 'What did you say?'

'I said, "*The Spider's Banquet,* will that do?" Why, what on earth's the matter?'

Doubtless you remember the score, Well-Versed Reader. The ballet describes the events in a Parisian garden dominated by a spider which waits for its prey. Two insects die in the web, but a praying mantis, at first worsted by the spider, finally kills the spider before it can enjoy its meal. It is thought that the composer used the story as a metaphor either for the gathering storm in Europe – we are in 1913 – or for the sovereignty of nature over humankind; but I saw in it a picture of my present case! I was the praying mantis: wounded but bouncing back; the insects who had fallen on to the web were the sad victims; the spider was the instigator of the entire sequence of events, brought in the end, as I hoped, to justice. I had been concentrating on the three male suspects. The important thing about Roussel's ballet, however, as far as I was concerned, is that the spider is female.

I sat there bemused, overcome with the suddenness and brilliance of this shaft of light. Beth's chance choice of music had enabled me to see the case in quite a different light. Should I ever have solved it otherwise? No wonder I have kept it concealed from Mr Falconer all these years! (He will have to read it after you have finished with the book.)

The following morning, I waited impatiently for Blundell to arrive. I could hardly contain myself.

'What is the name of Elspeth Fletcher's old boy-friend?' I asked.

'Rod Something-or-Other,' he said. 'Why?'

'Find him and arrest him. I want him here.'

'What's the charge, Inspector?'

'Murder of Audrey Fletcher, conspiracy to defraud, illegal disposal of a dead body: that'll do for a start.'

Blundell looked completely amazed. 'How do you figure that – Sir?'

'Just do as I say. I suddenly realised last night that this case has been like a spider's web. I now know who the spider is.'

And when Blundell left to pick up our Rod, I left to catch the spider.

Rod was an unattractive youth: gangly, awkward, shifty, with big hands and narrow eyes. He shambled into the interview room with fear and resignation printed on his unappealing features, but I felt only momentary pity for him. He was prey to forces stronger than himself - greed, lust – and he lacked the judgement and self-discipline to overcome them. Having given in to self-indulgence in his youth, when the testing-time came he was unable to extricate himself nobly. He was a pawn in the game and passes out of our story.

While Blundell was thus engaged, I and another sergeant sat in a neighbouring interview-room, tape-recorder playing.

'Elspeth,' I said, 'you know why you're here. You've led us a painful dance, but the time of reckoning has now arrived.'

She said nothing.

'Let me tell you what I think.'

There was no reaction.

'You overreached yourself, carried away with visions of wealth and the chance to enjoy it, but the people you used were not, fortunately, of the same mettle. There were two flaws in your scheme which were your undoing because of the people involved.'

I waited. Eventually she found the energy to ask, 'What?'

'Your first mistake was to suggest Angelo as your sister's accomplice. Oh, you were clever about it. You feigned reluctance, you painted him grey, not black, but you didn't take into account how he would come across at interview.'

'What do you mean?'

'I mean that he is an innocent: no one in their right mind would have chosen him to take part in a perilous and complex undertaking. He came across as honest and genuinely puzzled. At first I was surprised, even mystified, that he didn't know where the monastery was, but I now realise he has just no intellectual curiosity. Now if Angelo was out of the picture, there had to be another male, not just for the physical task of transporting Jadwiga's body, but to make the crucial phone-call to the abbot. The professor's voice might have been recognised. You would not have chosen anyone over whom you did not have complete control. Your father's dead, your brother you don't see very often. It had to be a boyfriend.'

She sat stonily. Eventually she said, 'And the second – "mistake", as you call it?'

'Well, it's not exactly a mistake, but again you didn't take into account how Jude would come across at interview.'

'Well, how did he come across?'

'As a sincere and devout monk, quite incapable of partaking in deception or jiggery-pokery.'

'So?'

'So when I asked him about a possible copy of the Hermann manuscript, I had to believe him when he told me that, to the best of his knowledge, there wasn't one. The abbot told me Brother Denis was the only monk of his acquaintance with the necessary skills to make it; Brother Jude had been a disciple and confidant of Brother Denis. If he said there wasn't one, the professor was lying. The so-called "missing quilisma" was a complete fabrication, but I'll come on to that again in a minute. Now Professor Dodsworth strikes me as self-satisfied and vainglorious, but I don't see him originating a scheme of this complexity. He is separated in both space and time from the main characters in the action, and I reckon he was tempted by a young relative. He's your mother's cousin, isn't he, or a great-uncle, or some such relation?'

'How did you find out?'

'Simple, only I should have thought of it a long time ago. On my way to pick you up from your work, I called in at the public library and consulted a copy of *Who's Who?*. I read, amongst all the professor's degrees, honorifics, awards, publications, clubs and so forth, the interesting detail that his mother's maiden name is Morton. You were foolish enough, you may remember, to give us your mother's maiden name – also Morton.'

'So where do I come into all this?'

'Well, let me go back to the beginning. This is how I see things. Jude reveals to Audrey, unsuspectingly, the existence of a valuable manuscript in the abbey's possession. She tells you, probably in all innocence, and you dream of the money it could bring you. You contact your great-uncle, or second-cousin, or whoever he is, whom you know to be an expert in matters of mediaeval manuscripts. The plan is this. Somehow – this part is not yet clear in your head – you intend to persuade the monastery to put the manuscript up for sale. Professor Dodsworth will buy it, money being no object at that moment, because he intends to recover his outlay; in fact, the more the merrier. He then shouts "Foul!" and claims off the auction-house, or perhaps the abbey.'

'And how is he going to manage all that?' Elspeth sneered.

'Simple. Once the manuscript is in his possession, he himself makes a copy, with or without the quilisma. My view is that the original has no quilisma and he added it in, but that is immaterial, because only he can tell the original from the copy. When, as he suspects I would, I ask to submit the manuscript to scientific tests, he gives me the original, which is naturally going to pass all the tests for antiquity. His copy was probably just as good, but he couldn't guarantee not to slip up somewhere. When his claim against the insurance company, or the abbey, is met in full, he has to hand over the copy – or at any rate, he fears he might – but the original is still in his possession. You see, he needed to convince us that he knew of only one manuscript – the copy. The existence of the original was to be kept concealed. At the same time, he couldn't make the copy so obviously a copy that the abbey or the auction-house or other potential buyers in the future would notice.'

'So where do I come into all this?'

'The reimbursed price of the manuscript comes to you, as the brains behind the scheme. All the professor is interested in is possessing the original Hermann manuscript without having to pay for it. He hands the proceeds over to you, and you set yourself and Rod up in the style to which you would like to be accustomed. Your problem was how to persuade the abbey to put the manuscript up for sale in the first place. I bet that a dozen schemes passed through your devious little mind before you hit on the idea of using poor Jadwiga's body.'

'You can't prove any of this.'

'Well, don't count on it. Experts are even now subjecting Rod's Austin-Healey to a detailed examination.'

'How do you know he's got an Austin-Healey?'

'I don't. I'm guessing. But I'm pretty sure I'm right. And they'll find traces of the knock that killed Audrey as well as evidence of Jadwiga in the boot. But let's focus on Jadwiga for the moment. This is my reconstruction. You were revolving multiple schemes in your pretty head, wondering how you could get the Hermann manuscript put on the open market. Not only was simply stealing it from the abbey very difficult, but it wouldn't net you the money it was worth: an unsellable manuscript is effectively worthless. You and Rod were returning home one evening when you chanced on a girl's body lying on the pavement. It took you only a few seconds to formulate a simple plan and execute it. You and Rod put the body into the boot of his car, together with the murder weapon that was lying on the pavement, and scarpered into the night. When you got the body home, you noticed the striking likeness between the girl and Audrey. This was lucky beyond your wildest hopes. If you had simply buried Jadwiga's body in the abbey cemetery, everybody would have wondered how it got there, and suspicion would not easily have fallen on the monks. So you dressed the body in some of Audrey's clothes and persuaded Audrey, probably with the incentive of a new life funded with the professor's money, to do a vanishing act. Now the body had every appearance of being that of someone known to have visited the abbey on a perfectly valid pretext and never to have been seen alive again. It was child's play thereafter to phone the abbey threatening to reveal the identity of the killer-monk and forcing the abbey to agree to a sale of the manuscript. The fact that Jude voted against the projected sale proves again, more or less, that he had nothing to do with your scheme.'

'If you're so clever, Inspector, why would I insist on having the proceeds given to a named charity? Wouldn't it have been much simpler for the proceeds to go to the abbey: much easier "to recover", wouldn't you say?'

'Yes, I've thought about that. I've come up with two possibilities. The first is that you thought you would spread the range of options for recovery of the auction money: three parties instead of two. The second is that it increased the publicity – the press-coverage – of the entire transaction, in the hope of putting additional pressure on the parties to cough up. Am I right on either count?'

'No, you're not, Inspector. It was Audrey's idea. I thought it was silly, but she insisted. She imagined that the abbey would have to go back to the charity to recover the money so that it could be returned to Professor Dodsworth. This, she said, would put the abbey in a bad light with the public: that was her motive.'

'I see,' I commented, viewing this new perspective on the matter with considerable disfavour. I ploughed on.

'Now let me come on to the most serious part of this whole scheme. I suspect that Audrey became importunate. Perhaps she demanded more than she had been promised. Perhaps she threatened to expose you and your grubby little scheme because she could no longer stomach leading a concealed life. Either way, she had to be eliminated. It could be, of course, that you simply resented handing over to her any share of the proceeds of the insurance scam and had intended from the very start to get rid of her. On an evening when you knew where she'd be at what time, Rod waited outside her house, or up the street, and as she came round the corner, he ran her down. That's murder, Elspeth, and you're in it up to your neck. Perhaps Audrey deserved to die. Perhaps she was a conniving little schemer, like yourself; perhaps she lacked a conscience and used Angelo. Perhaps she didn't. But murder is murder.

'Let me move on to the burglary at the professor's house. This was necessary because the auction-house wouldn't stump up a refund and the abbey wasn't able to -- not at that juncture, anyway. Dodsworth could hardly challenge a worthy charity in public to get his money back: he would have lost face. So he burgles himself, or gets the egregious Rod to burgle him. Not difficult. He is then in a position to claim off the insurance. He would have to hope that the company would accept that he had lost the original and not make inquiries of the police. The insurance company is in Lincoln; the police are in Warwick: why should they collude? In any case, he has no choice. I bet you were threatening him with all sorts of dire consequences unless he produced pronto the money he owed you. He couldn't put the original up for sale again, because that would be to reveal his part in your underhand doings. The burglary seemed an easier option than putting pressure on the abbey to claim off the charity.'

I left Elspeth pondering these things. Her future was not rosy. In the meantime, I phoned Professor Dodsworth to ask him to present himself at the Lincoln police-station, where I should be charging him formally. I had a few things to sort out in Warwick before making my meagre preparations for an hour and a half's drive to Lincoln, but before I had set off, I had a phone-call. Mrs Dodsworth had phoned the police to say that her husband had hanged himself in his garage, and he had left a letter for me. I asked the officer who informed me to read it out over the phone.

Dear Inspector Wickfield (I heard).

I shall be gone when you read this. That is no loss, I hear you say, and you are right. I simply cannot live with the shame I have brought on myself and my profession. I should like to make the following statement. I charge Elspeth with being the instigator of the whole ugly matter, but then you are sure to know that already, so it is not news, and it does not in the slightest excuse me for my part.

Elspeth phoned me to ask whether I should be interested in "acquiring" the Hermann manuscript for my private collection. Some publicity would be required, but I should not have to part with any money, except in the first instance. I couldn't resist the bait thus dangled. I agreed to buy the manuscript at auction, to pretend I had purchased a copy, to recover my money off the abbey and hand the sum over to Elspeth. What she did with it was her own concern. I should possess the original, and I should increase my reputation for discernment, taste and financial means.

Unfortunately, I had not foreseen that neither the auction-house nor the abbey would be willing to reimburse me. Naïve? Probably. I was blinded by the thought of possessing the Hermann manuscript. I was therefore forced to go back to Elspeth and request help in setting up a burglary without my wife's foreknowledge. I might have got away with it, only you forestalled me with your phone-call and made it impossible for me to continue.

I wish you to know that I intend to make restitution for my misdeeds, in so far as I can. The original Hermann manuscript is in my safe, together with the copy I confess to having made once the original manuscript was in my possession. I had long possessed ancient parchment, given me at Westvleteren Abbey, which no longer had a need for it, and I had over the years acquired sufficient skills and materials to produce a passable imitation. The original manuscript is the one *without* the quilisma. I gladly bequeath it -- them - to the Abbey of Our Lady of the Snows, with the wish that the copy might be put somewhere on permanent display, perhaps in an accessible public collection. The original is without doubt a marvellous work of art wrought by a spiritual master. Don't think too unkindly of me, Inspector.

Yours with profound sorrow

Theobald Dodsworth.

Hamlet's words came to mind:

> The dram of evil
> Doth all the noble substance of a doubt
> To his own scandal.

I have always taken them to mean that an atom of malpractice can make even a noble person fear scandal. The professor had devoted himself to noble things in his lifetime, but he had corrupted his integrity by stooping to Elspeth's schemes. He could not thereafter live with his conscience.

POSTSCRIPT

There is a somewhat curious sequel to this story, which, if you will bear with me, I shall now relate. The glamorous Elspeth and young Rod paid the final price for their conspiracy; and I felt sorry for Blundell. The professor, as already related, was dead, by his own hand. I have no idea what happened to the luckless Angelo. Brother Jude, I think – I know – continued at the monastery, deep in prayer and the things of God. The surface of the monastic waters, disturbed by such vehement waves, subsided as time went on, and with the passing of Brother Denis, the only person with any claim to inside knowledge – or perhaps inside ignorance would be a more fitting phrase - the upset over the Hermann manuscript faded from active memory.

However, a few years later, a paragraph in a national newspaper caught my eye. I reproduce it here:

> The curator of the National Museum of Mediaeval Manuscripts and Incunabula, in London's dockland, Mr George Harbin, said he was shocked at the damage caused by a fire in the Museum last night. Local residents, seeing flames issuing from the building, had contacted the fire-brigade, and the blaze was quickly brought under control. However, this morning, when inspection was possible, Mr Harbin said that an entire room of precious manuscripts had been destroyed in the flames. One particularly sad loss, he said, was the museum's prize exhibit, the so-called Hermann Anthem. The fire is believed to have been started by an electrical fault.

Wondering whether the abbot of Our Lady of the Snows had seen this item of news – probably not – and whether the museum authorities had yet informed him – possibly – I gave the abbot a ring, to offer my condolences on the loss of their manuscript. Fr Donatus appreciated my contact and suggested I come to the abbey for Mass on Sunday and stay afterwards for a coffee with him; he had a matter he wished to communicate to me. To this I agreed. Beth accompanied me.

It was a mild spring day when Beth and I, for the first time since the events surrounding the sale of the Hermann manuscript, drove slowly up the Cass Valley. Its beauty never wearied me, and I envied the monks who lived there, in a veritable Garden of Eden remote from the bustle of the surrounding towns. The deciduous trees were bright green with new buds, and the first of the abbey's crops were poking above the ploughed and sown soil. We were the only visitors that Sunday, and we felt a little conspicuous in the nave when everyone else was in the choir. The service had a soothing effect. The monks did not sing *Alma Redemptoris Mater.*

'You know, Inspector,' the abbot said, when we were settled in the familiar Blue Parlour afterwards, with a pot of tea and a small plate of biscuits – 'and Mrs Wickfield, of course' – turning to Beth – 'we couldn't decide whether to keep the original manuscript here, safe, or at least more or less safe, in the bowels of the abbey and loan the copy for permanent exhibition in London, or the other way round. We discussed this in chapter. Some of the brothers said that the insurance of the original was beyond us and should be the responsibility of the museum: we should keep only the copy. Others were unhappy about letting the original out of our sight and maintained that we should loan the copy. In the end, we gave the original to the museum, and that is the one that has apparently been destroyed. The museum phoned me the same day that you did, to impart the sad news.'

I felt there was more to come, and I was not disappointed.

'However, as you know, we were confused by the late Professor Dodsworth as to which was the original and which the copy. The first story was that the original contained the famous – or infamous – quilisma and that the copy was known to be such because it lacked it.

It then transpired that there was no copy at all until after the auction, and we then had to depend entirely on the professor's statement in his suicide note that the original contained the quilisma all the time. Now put yourself in the professor's shoes. He wished to make amends for trying to rob the abbey of our good reputation or for forcing us to approach Christians for Justice for our money back. He also asked us to exhibit, or at least make readily available to scholars, one or other of the manuscripts. Did he imagine that we would expose the original or the copy? Did he bluff, double-bluff or treble-bluff by telling us that the original manuscript had the quilisma? Did he think the original would be safer with us or in a museum?'

'I think I follow you,' I said. 'You're telling me that you're now unsure which of the two manuscripts was destroyed in the fire.'

'Precisely!'

'What would the Blessed Hermann say to that?'

'I'm not sure the Blessed Hermann would care one way or the other.' He paused with what looked remarkably like a twinkle in his monkish eye. 'And I'll tell you something else, Inspector: I'm not sure, after all the trouble last time, that we do either!'